ATTACK OF THE MUTANT LUNCH LADY

Librarian Reviewer
Katharine Kan
Graphic novel reviewer and Library Consultant, Panama City, FL
MLS in Library and Information Studies, University of Hawaii at
Manoa, HI

Reading Consultant
Elizabeth Stedem
Educator/Consultant, Colorado Springs, CO
MA in Elementary Education, University of Denver, CO

Graphic Sparks are published by Stone Arch Books,
A Capstone Imprint
1710 Roe Crest Drive
North Mankato, Minnesota 56003
www.capstonepub.com

Library of Congress Cataloging-in-Publication Data
Nickel, Scott.
    Attack of the Mutant Lunch Lady: A Buzz Beaker Brainstorm / by Scott Nickel;
illustrated by Andy J Smith.
        p. cm. — (Graphic Sparks—A Buzz Beaker Brainstorm)
        ISBN 978-1-4342-0451-6 (library binding)
        ISBN 978-1-4342-0501-8 (paperback)
        1. Graphic novels. I. Smith, Andy J., 1975– II. Title.
PN6727.N544A88 2008
741.5'973—dc22   2007031250

Summary: Brainy Buzz Beaker thought nothing could be grosser than cafeteria food.
That's before the school's lunch lady turned into a mutant blob of mystery meat. Now,
Buzz and his best friend, Larry, must discover a way to stop the Cafeteria Creature.

Art Director: Heather Kindseth
Graphic Designer: Brann Garvey

Printed in the United States of America in North Mankato, Minnesota.
042014
008142R

ATTACK OF THE MUTANT LUNCH LADY

written by SCOTT NICKEL

illustrated by ANDY J. SMITH

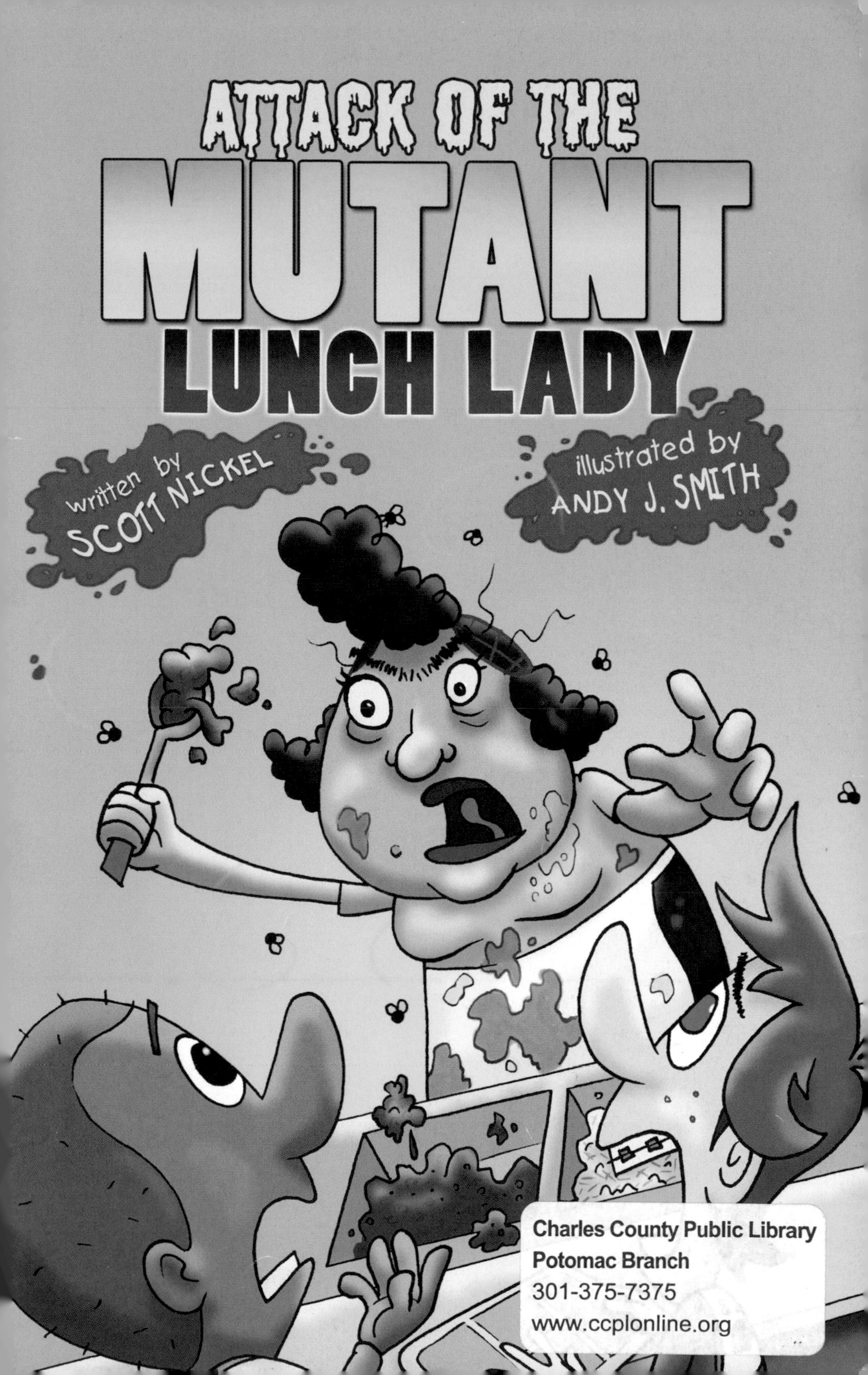

CAST OF CHARACTERS

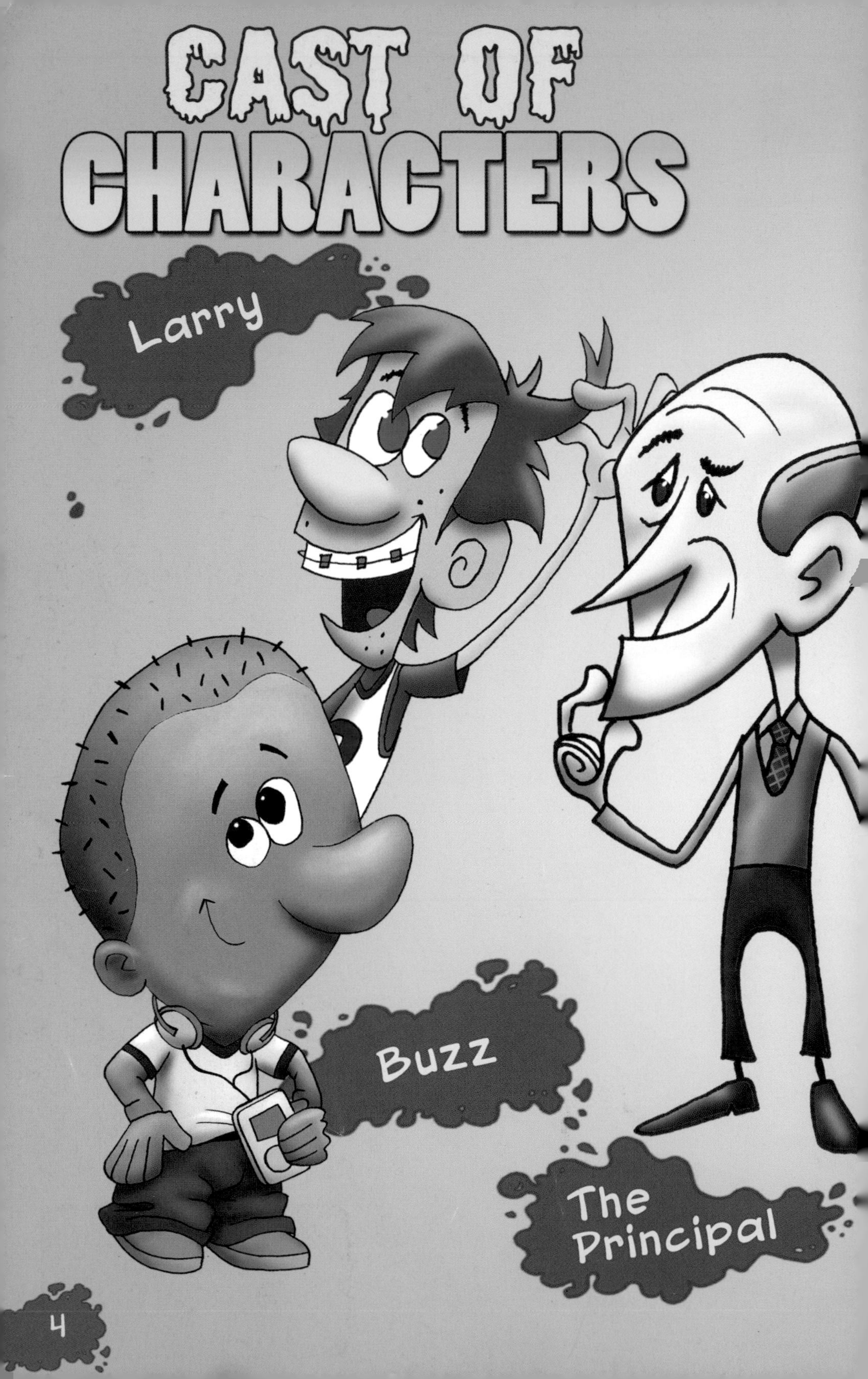
Larry
Buzz
The Principal

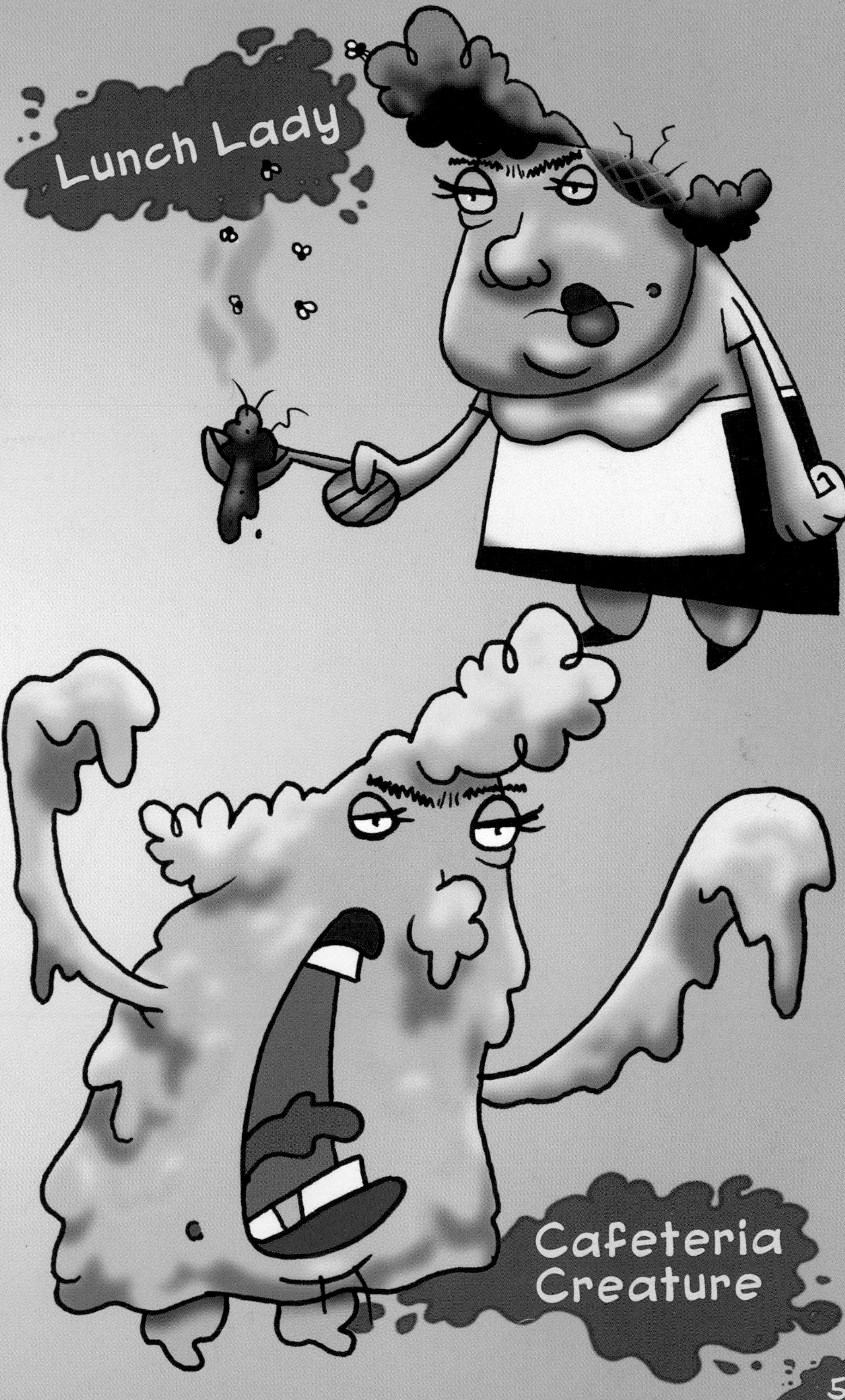
Lunch Lady
Cafeteria
Creature

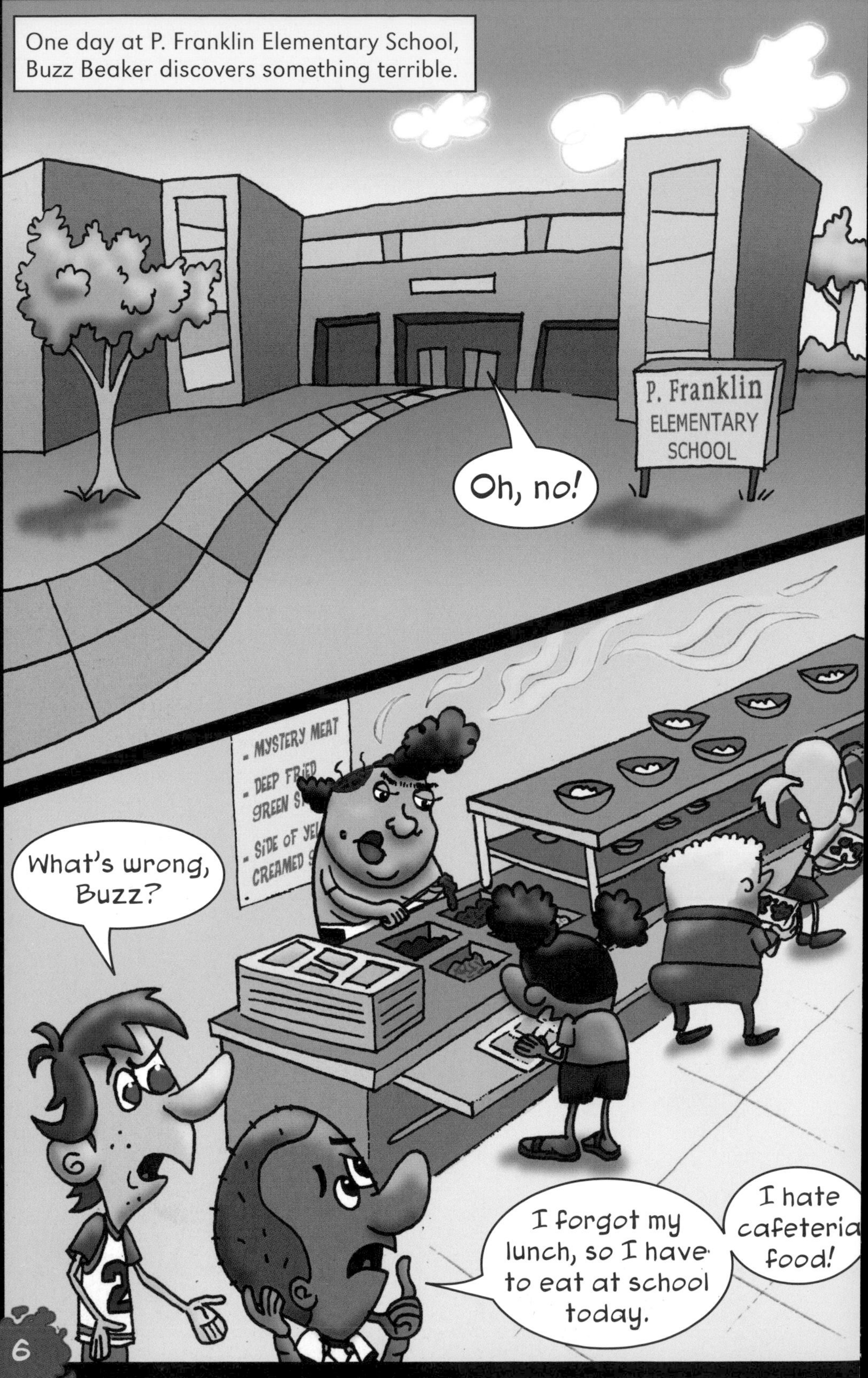
One day at P. Franklin Elementary School, Buzz Beaker discovers something terrible.
P. Franklin ELEMENTARY SCHOOL
Oh, no!
- MYSTERY MEAT
What's wrong, Buzz?
I forgot my lunch, so I have to eat at school today.
I hate cafeteria food!

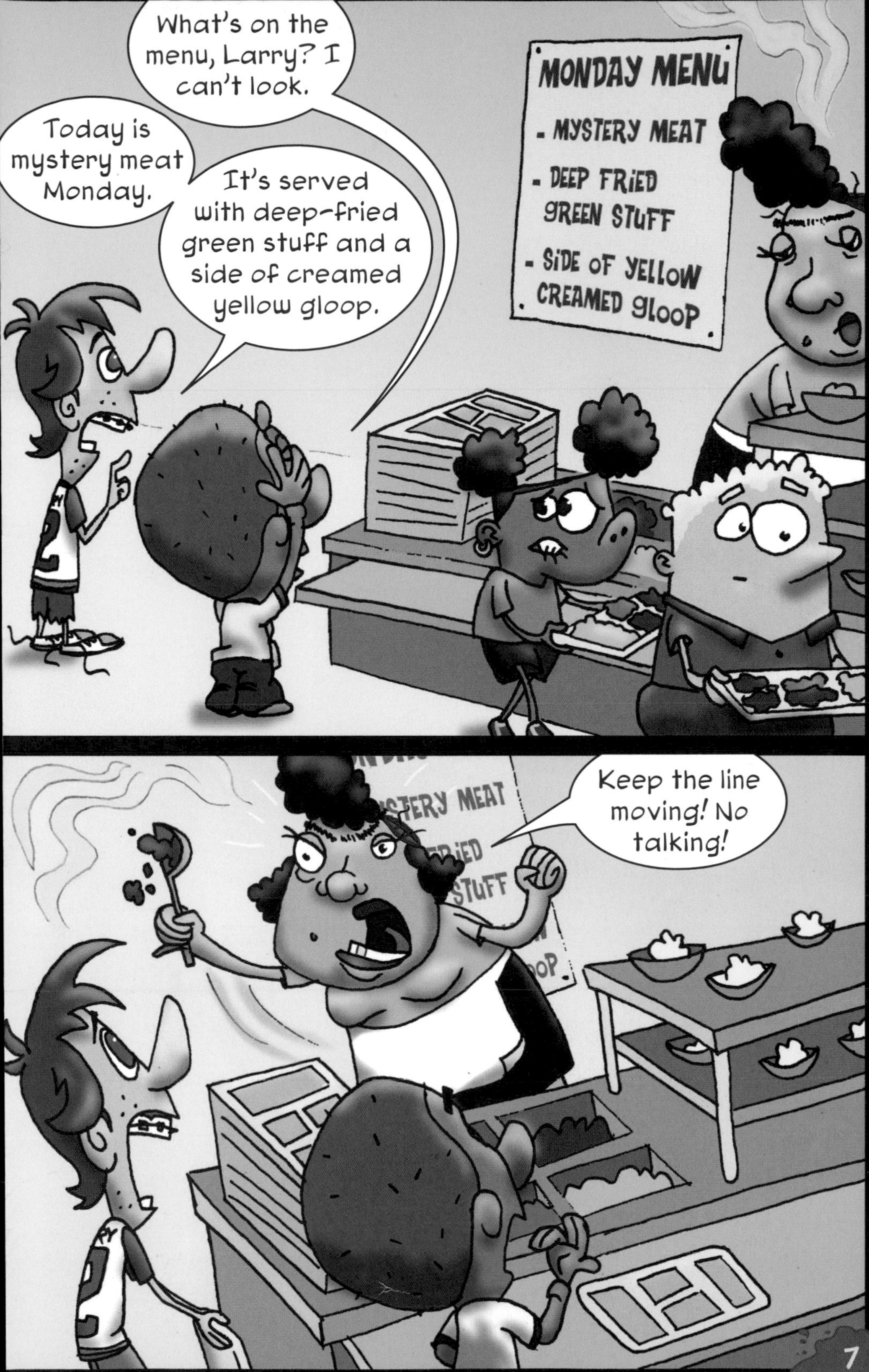
What's on the menu, Larry? I can't look.
Today is mystery meat Monday.
It's served with deep-fried green stuff and a side of creamed yellow gloop.
MONDAY MENU
- MYSTERY MEAT
- DEEP FRIED GREEN STUFF
- SIDE OF YELLOW CREAMED GLOOP
Keep the line moving! No talking!

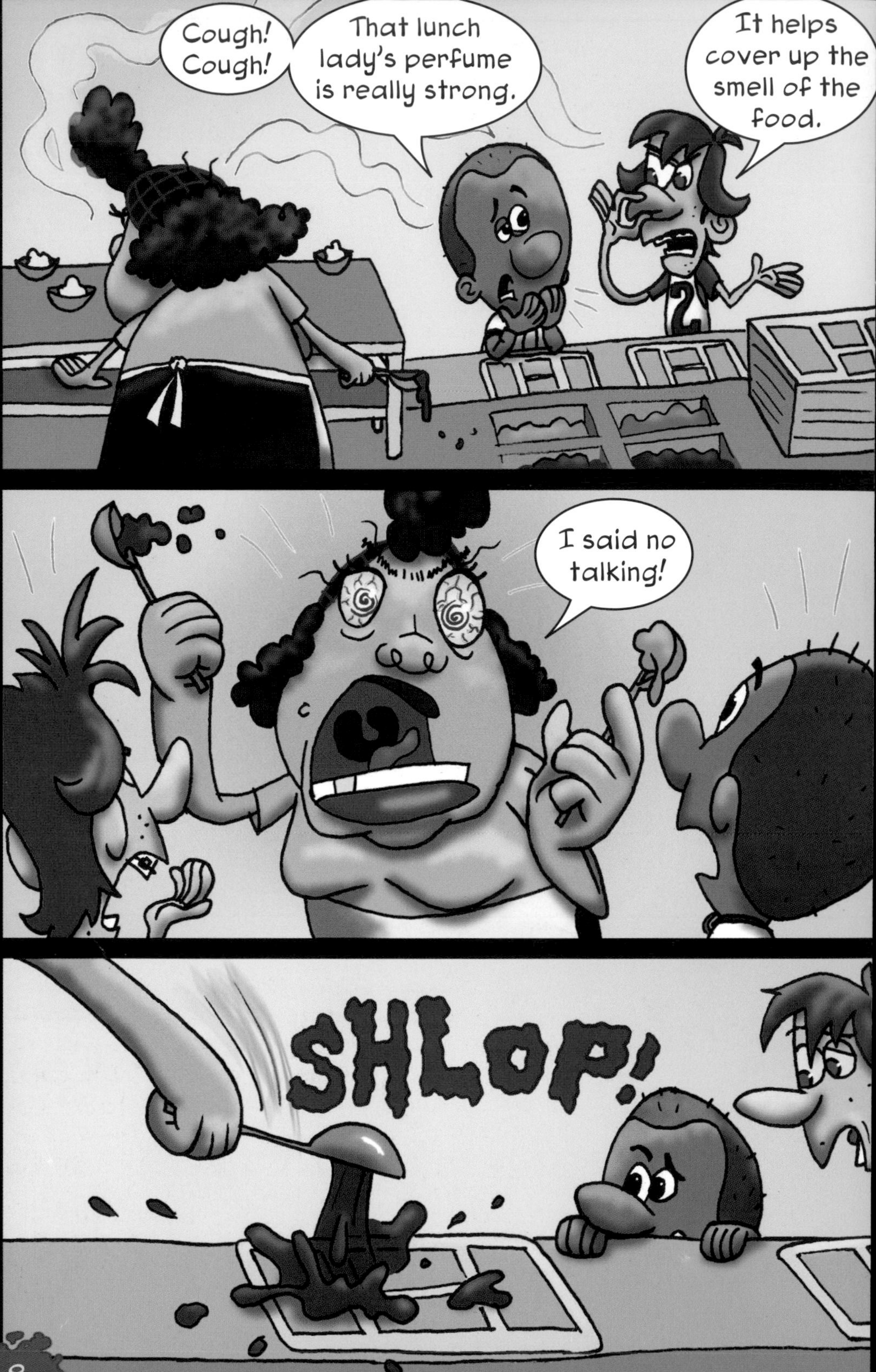

Cough! Cough!
That lunch lady's perfume is really strong.
It helps cover up the smell of the food.
I said no talking!
SHLOP!

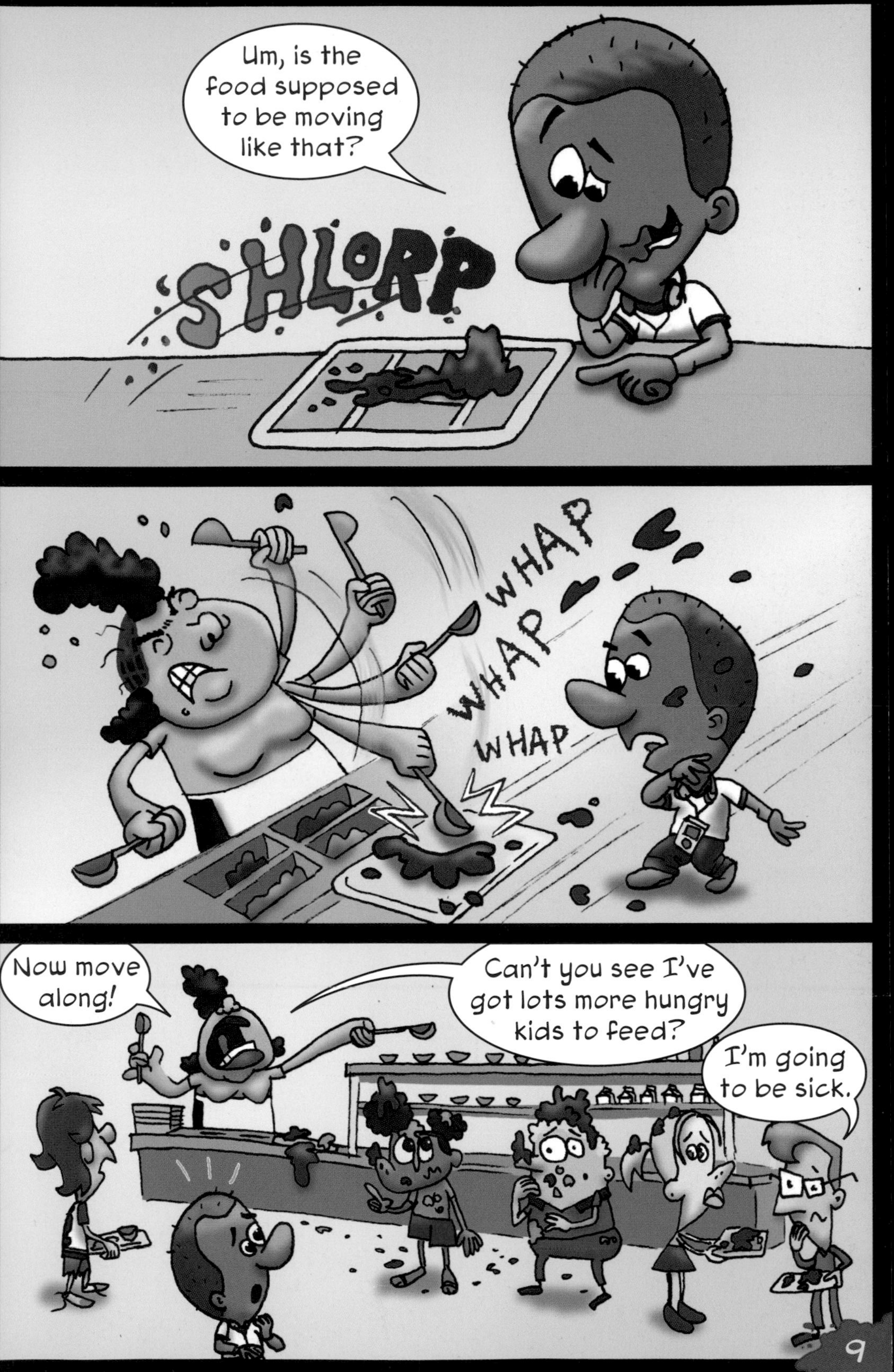
Um, is the food supposed to be moving like that?
SHLORP
WHAP
WHAP
WHAP
Now move along!
Can't you see I've got lots more hungry kids to feed?
I'm going to be sick.

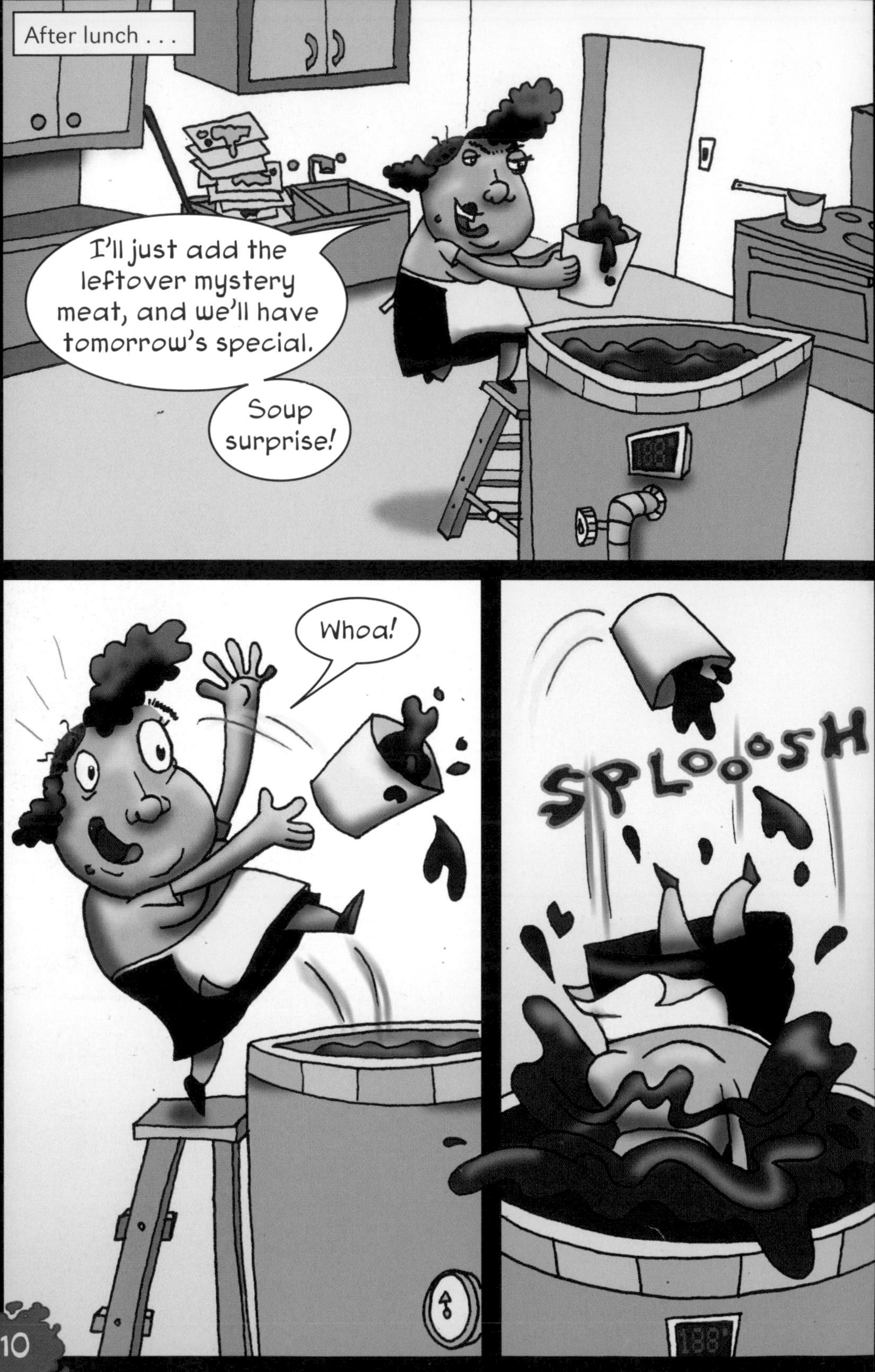
After lunch . . .
I'll just add the leftover mystery meat, and we'll have tomorrow's special.
Soup surprise!
Whoa!
SPLOOOOSH

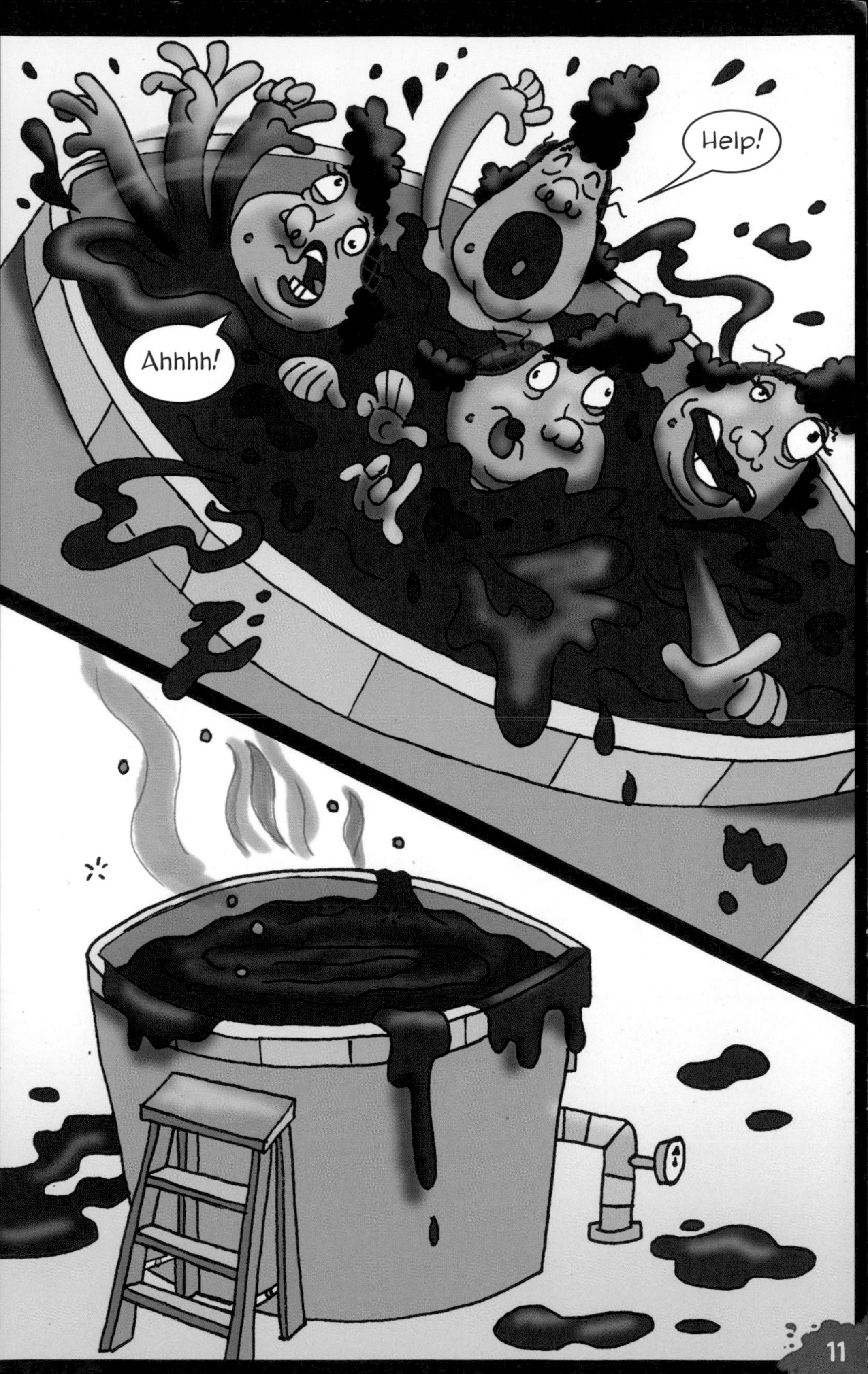
Help!
Ahhhh!

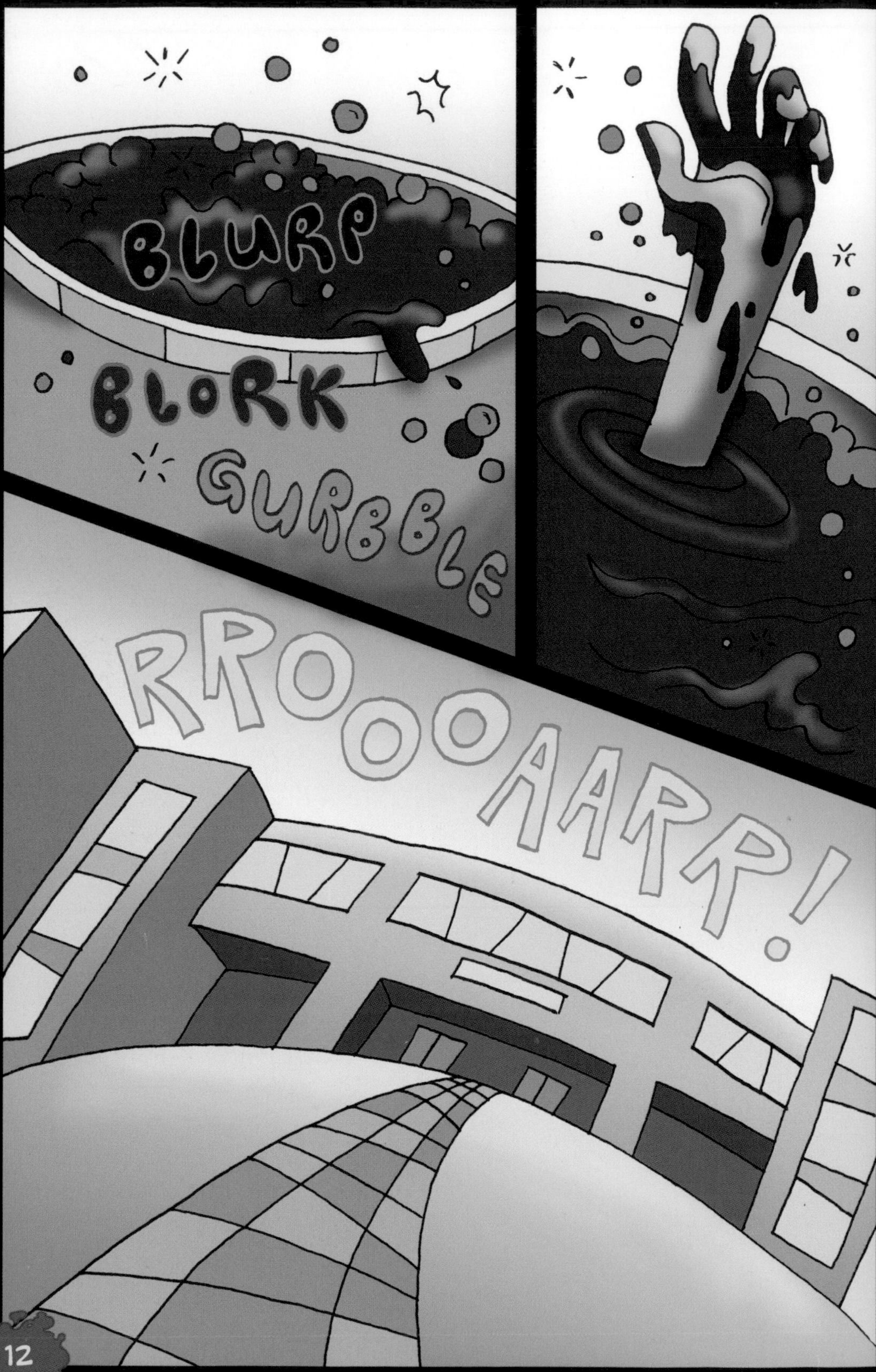
BLURP
BLORK
GURBBLE
RROOOAARR!

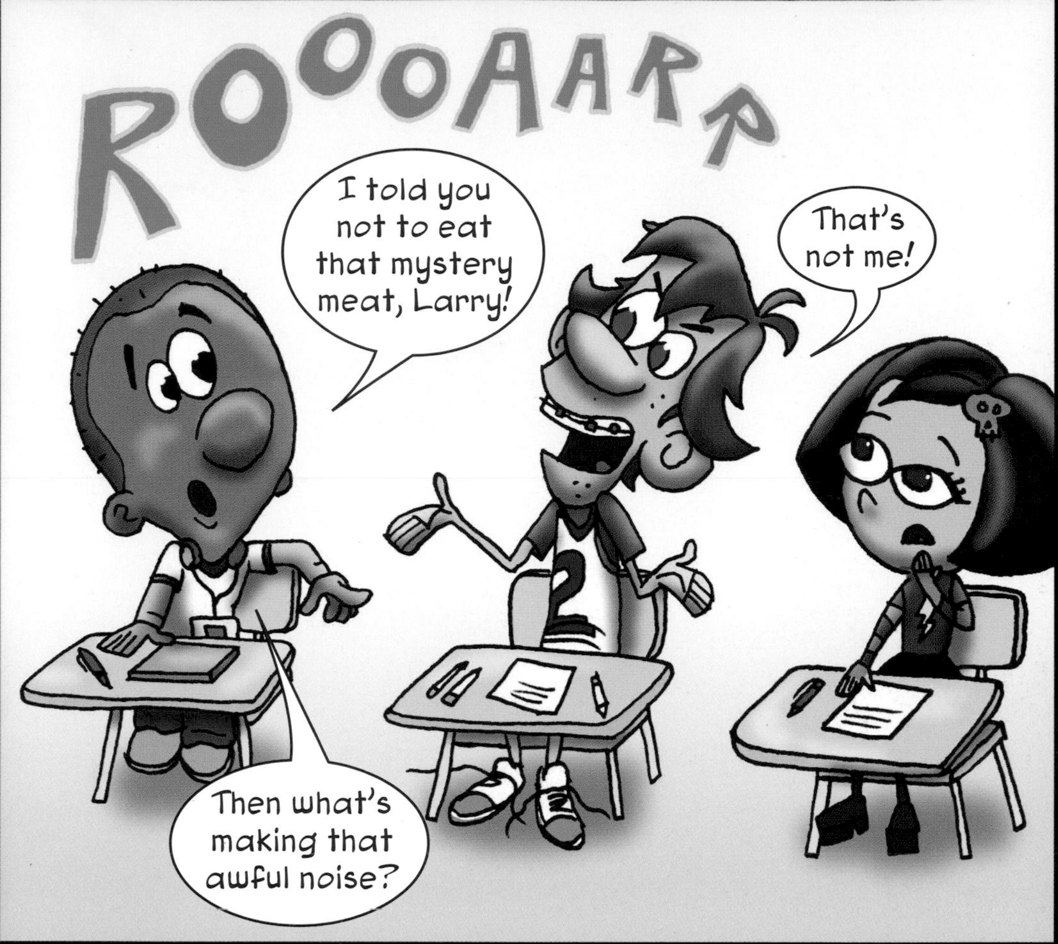
ROOOAARR
I told you not to eat that mystery meat, Larry!
That's not me!
Then what's making that awful noise?

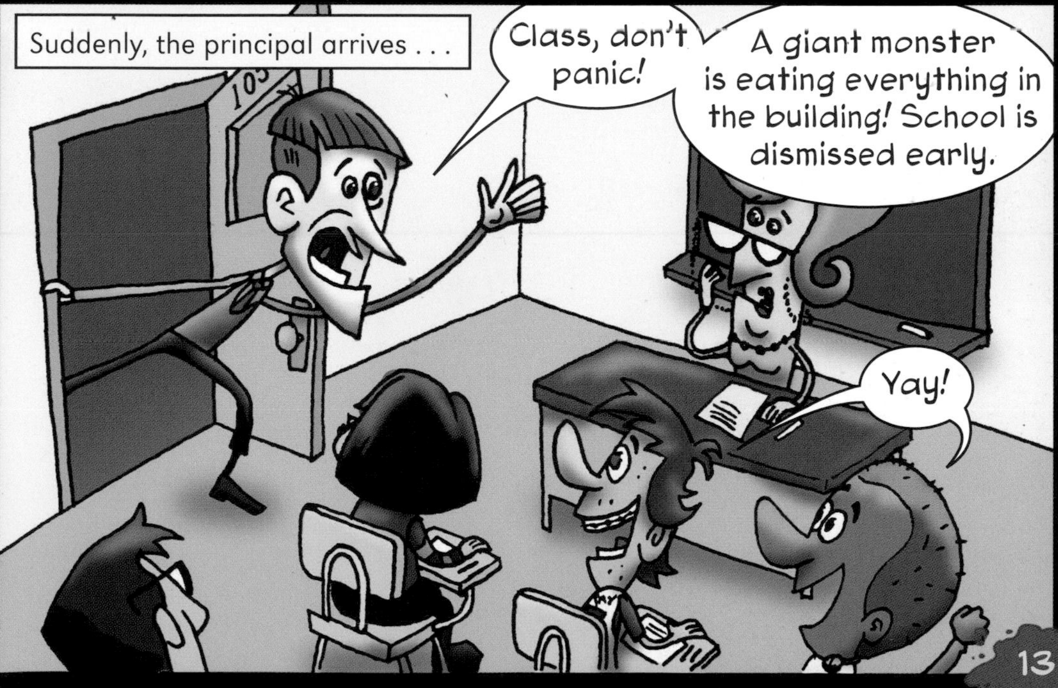
Suddenly, the principal arrives . . .
105
Class, don't panic!
A giant monster is eating everything in the building! School is dismissed early.
Yay!

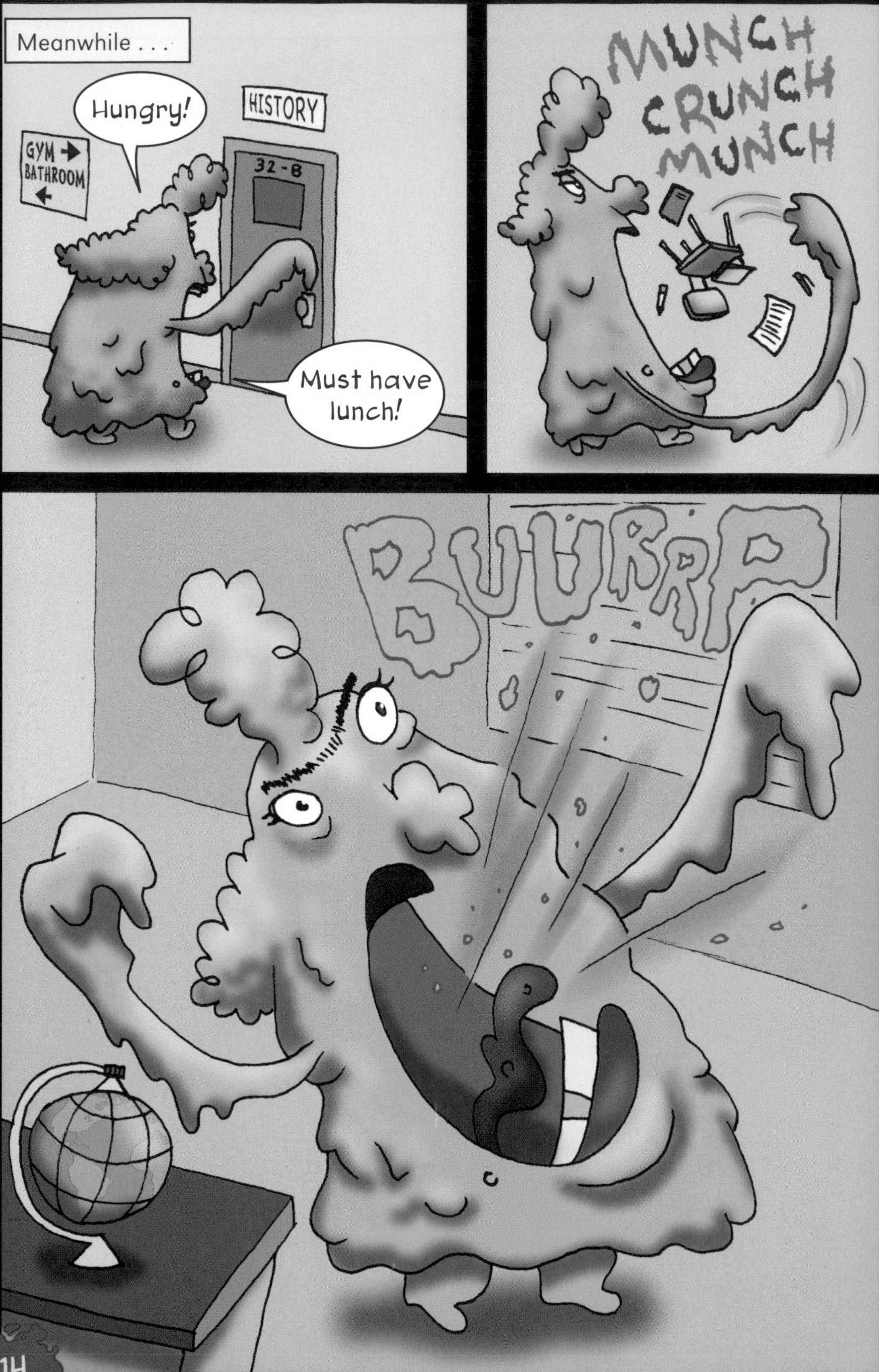
Meanwhile . . .
Hungry!
HISTORY
GYM
BATHROOM
32-B
Must have lunch!
MUNCH
CRUNCH
MUNCH
BUURRP

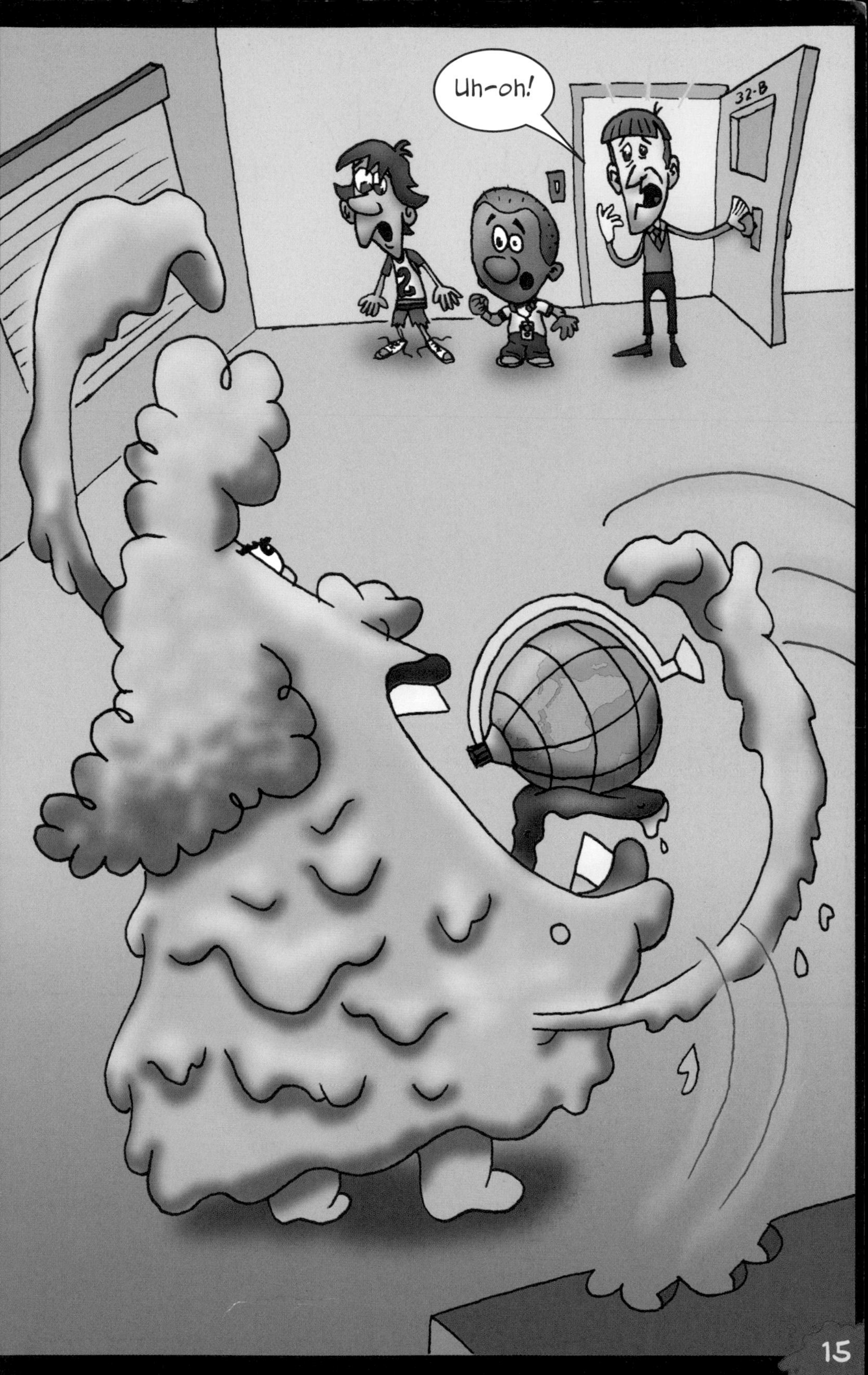
Uh-oh!
32-B

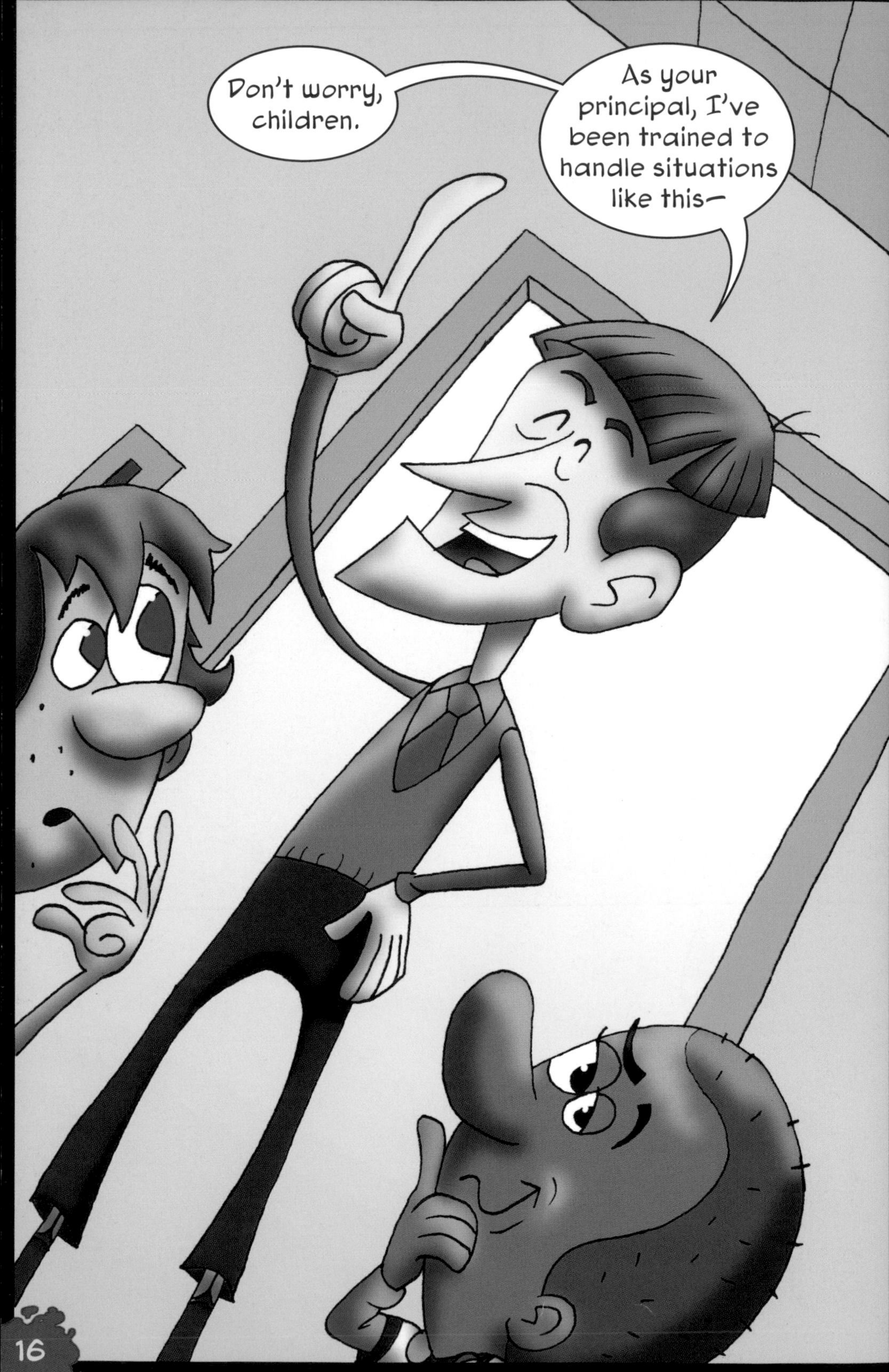
Don't worry, children.
As your principal, I've been trained to handle situations like this—

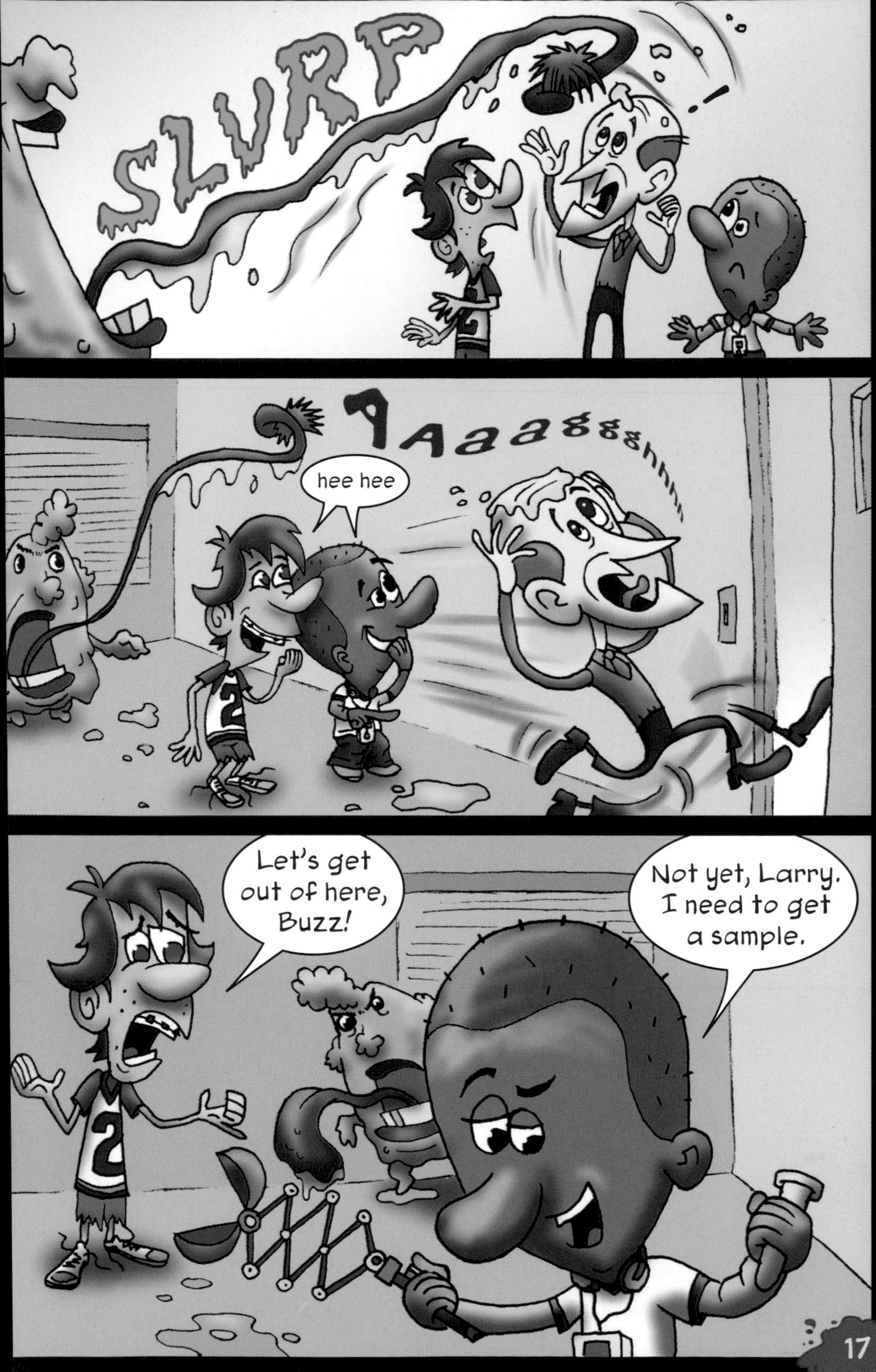
SLURP
Aaaaggghhhh
hee hee
Let's get out of here, Buzz!
Not yet, Larry. I need to get a sample.

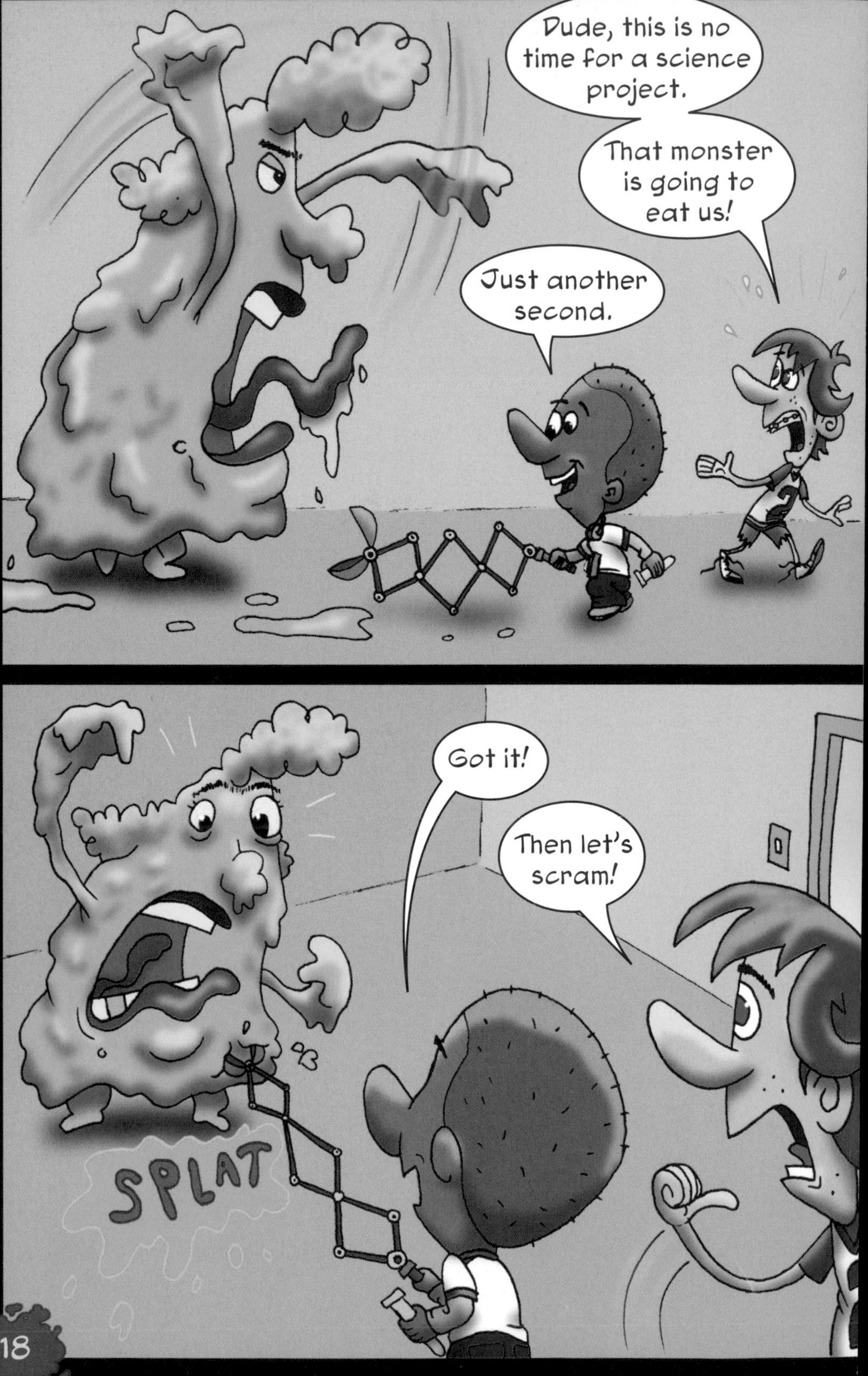
Dude, this is no time for a science project.
That monster is going to eat us!
Just another second.
Got it!
Then let's scram!
SPLAT

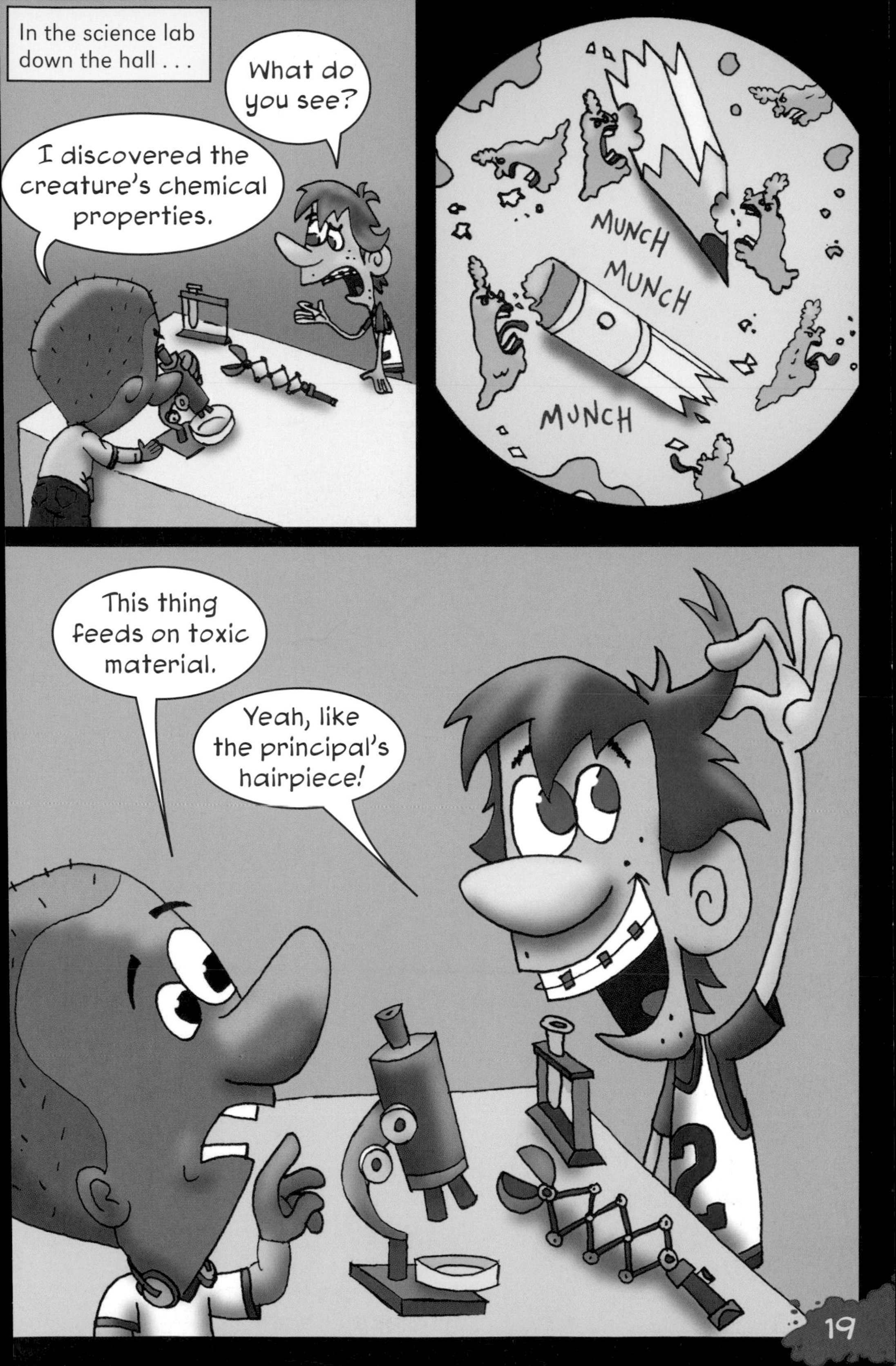

In the science lab down the hall . . .
What do you see?
I discovered the creature's chemical properties.
MUNCH
MUNCH
MUNCH
This thing feeds on toxic material.
Yeah, like the principal's hairpiece!

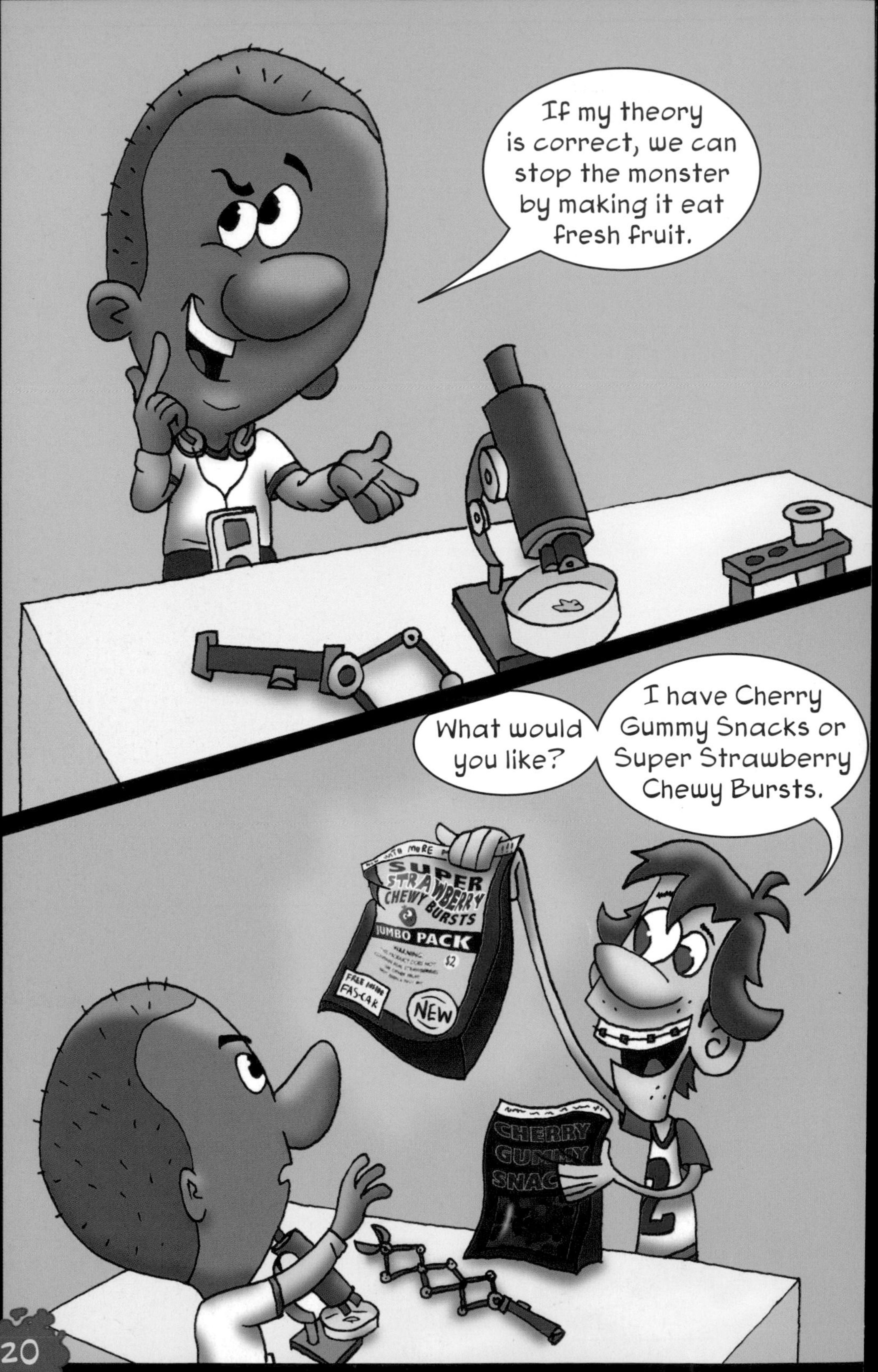
If my theory is correct, we can stop the monster by making it eat fresh fruit.
What would you like?
I have Cherry Gummy Snacks or Super Strawberry Chewy Bursts.
SUPER STRAWBERRY CHEWY BURSTS
JUMBO PACK
$2
NEW
CHERRY GUMMY SNAC

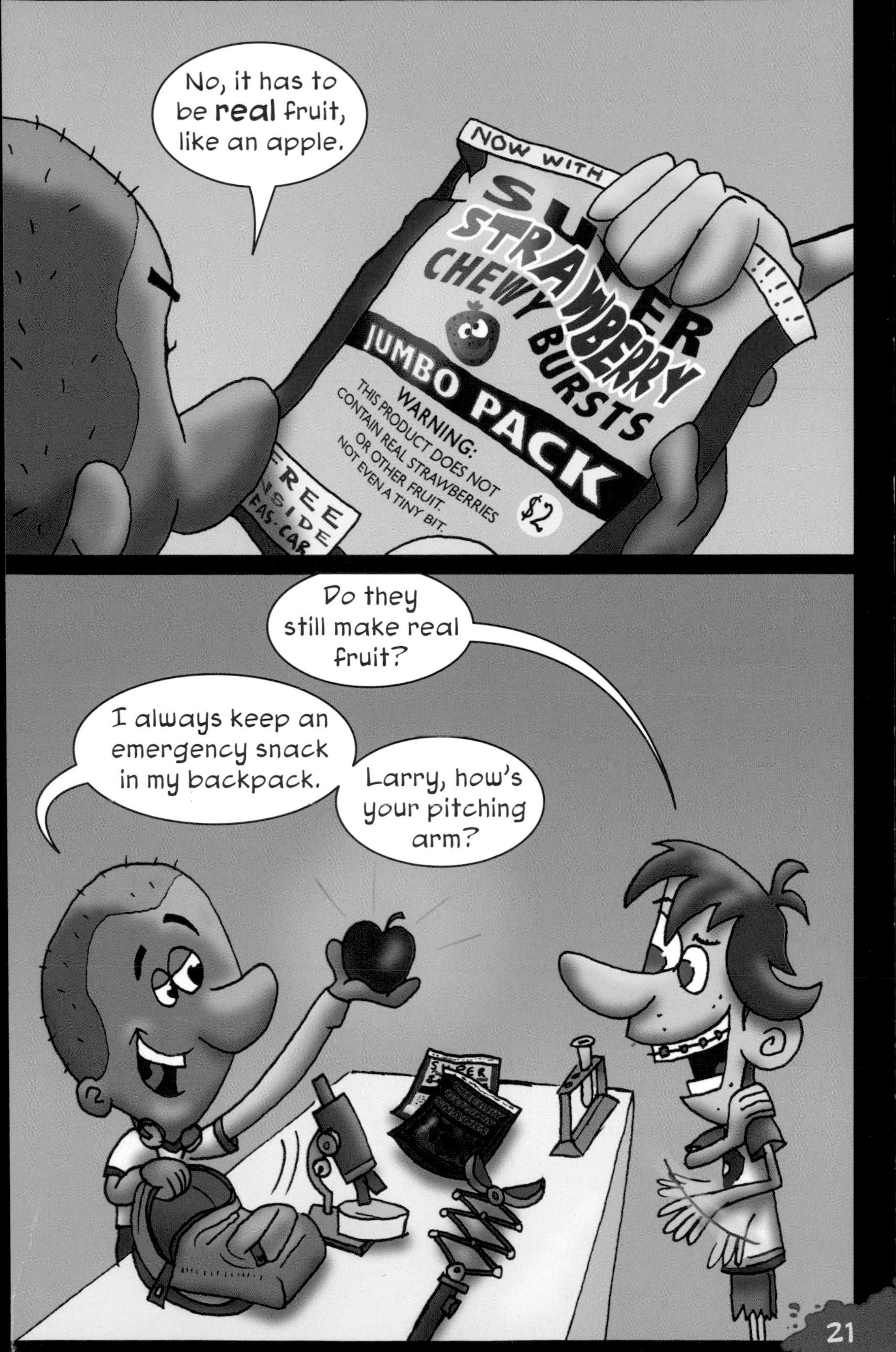
No, it has to be **real** fruit, like an apple.
NOW WITH
SUPER
STRAWBERRY
CHEWY BURSTS
JUMBO PACK
WARNING:
THIS PRODUCT DOES NOT
CONTAIN REAL STRAWBERRIES
OR OTHER FRUIT.
NOT EVEN A TINY BIT.
$2
FREE
Do they still make real fruit?
I always keep an emergency snack in my backpack.
Larry, how's your pitching arm?

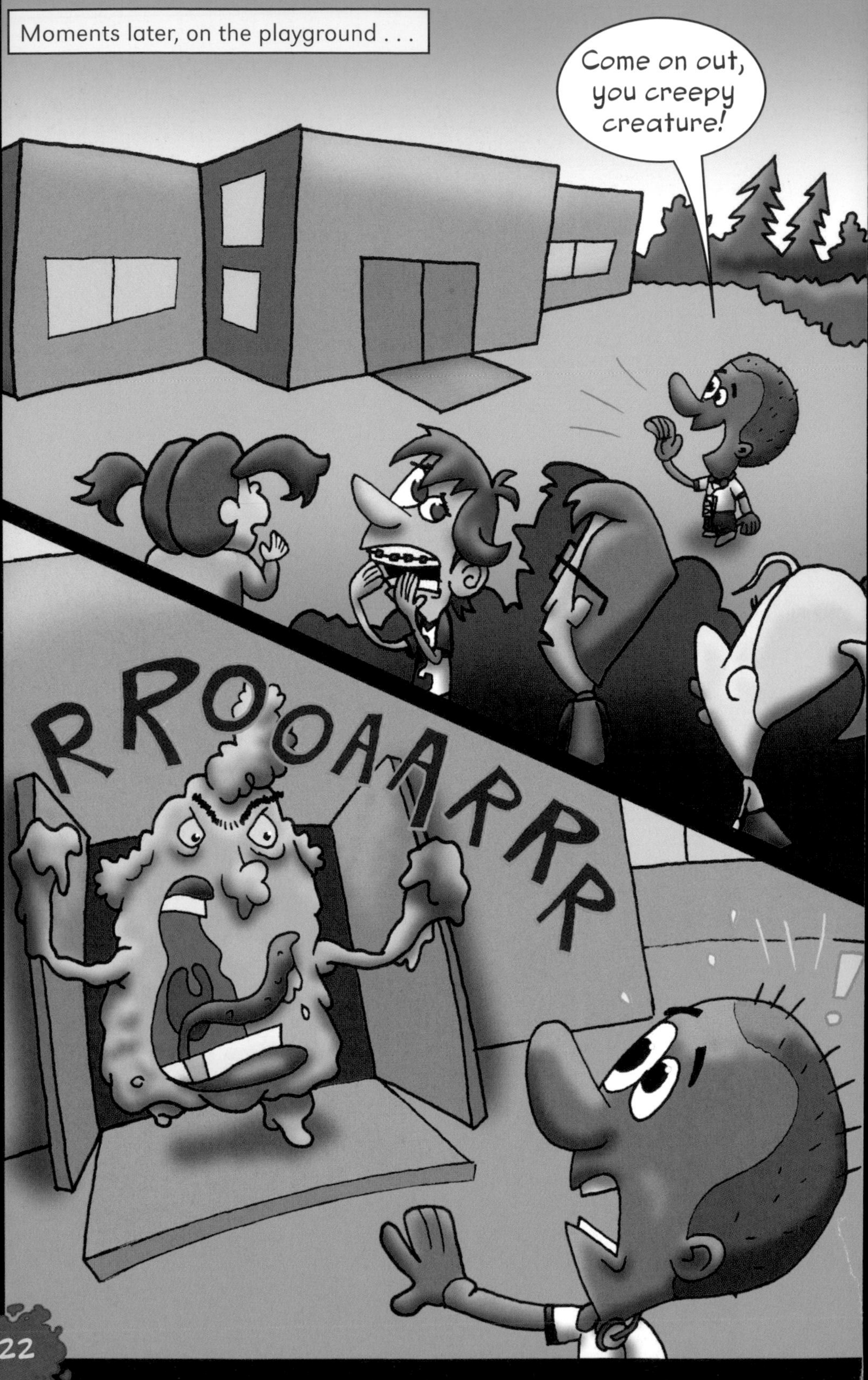

Moments later, on the playground . . .
Come on out, you creepy creature!
RROOAARRR

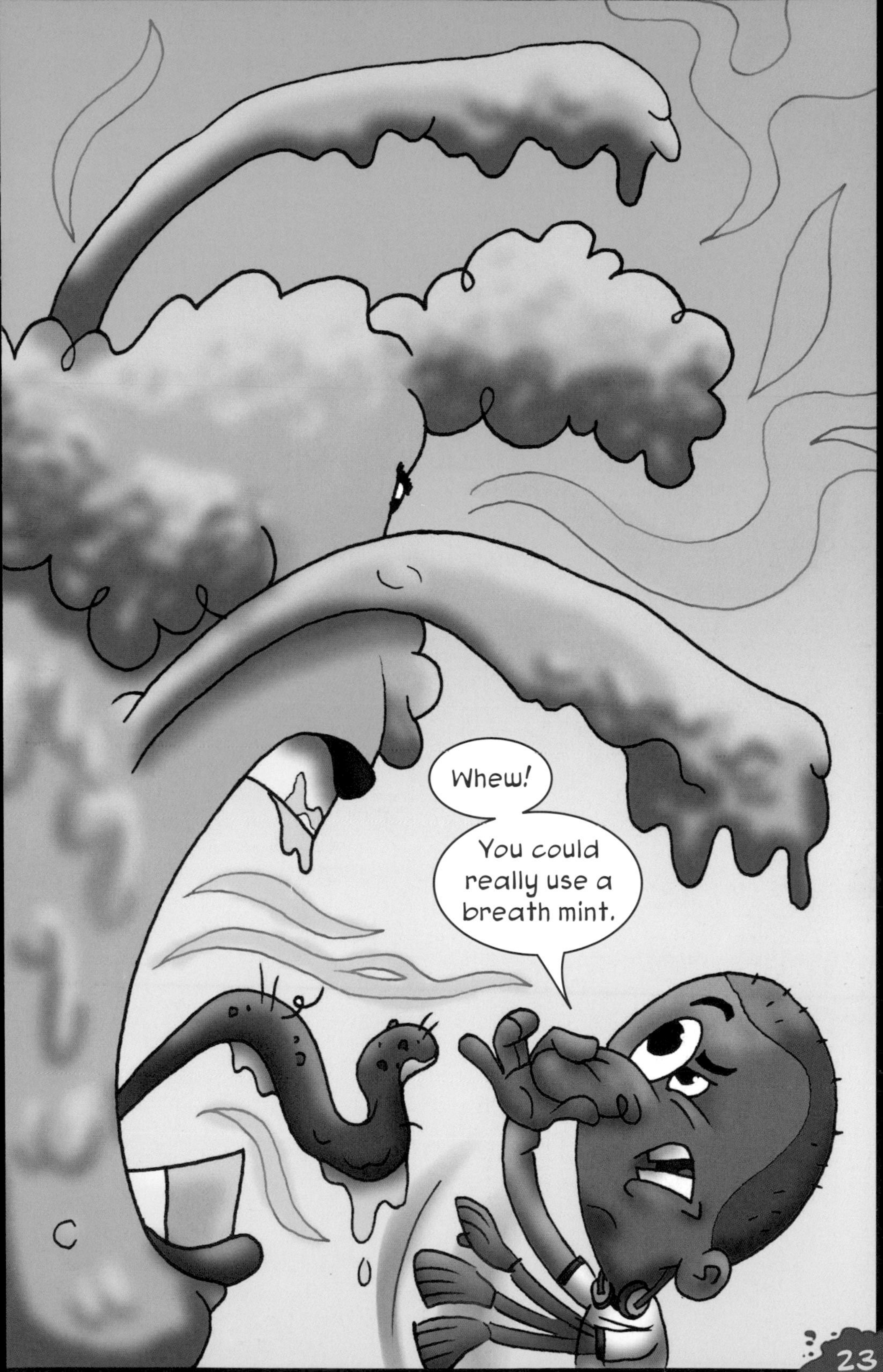
Whew!
You could really use a breath mint.

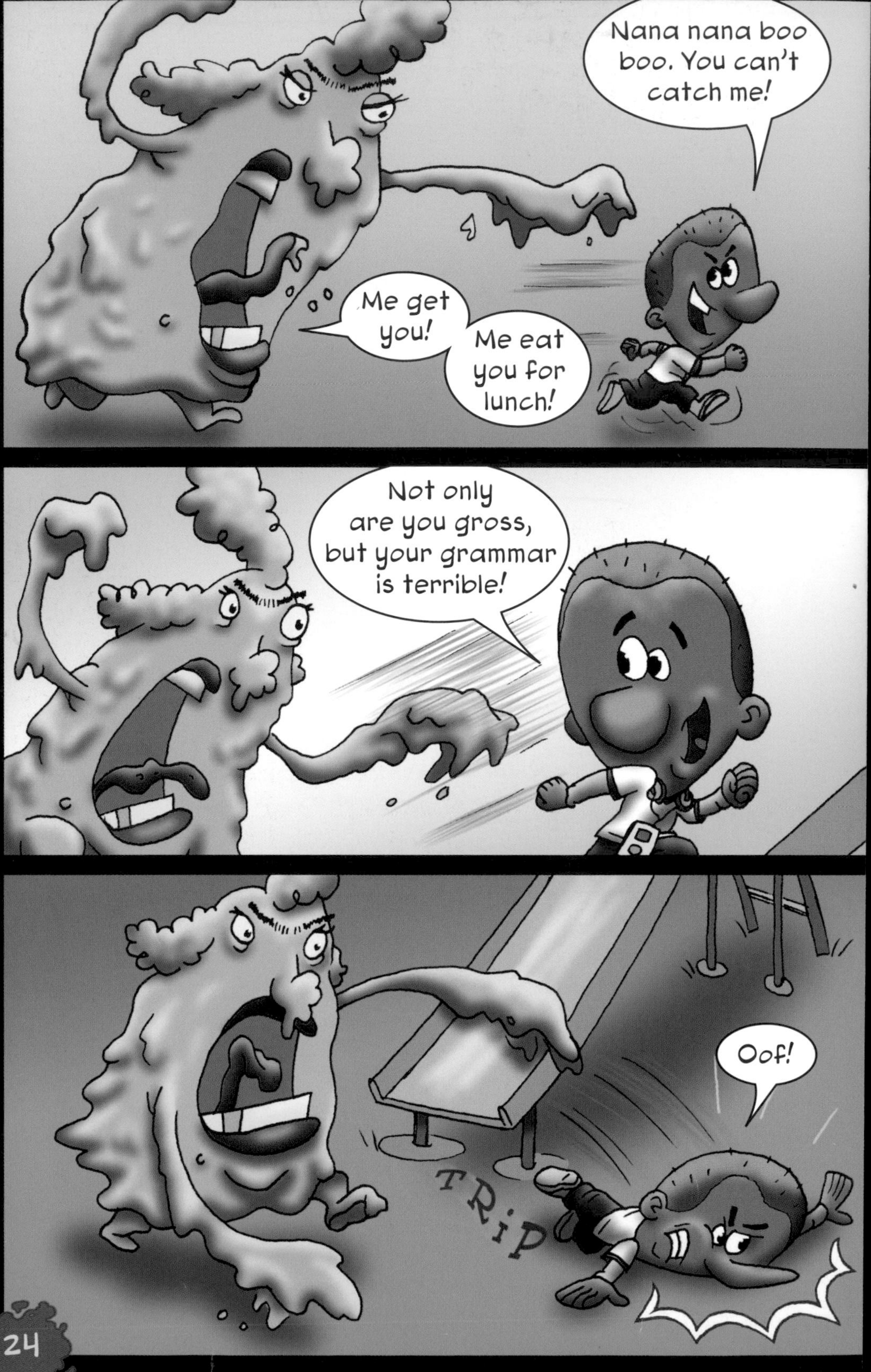
Nana nana boo boo. You can't catch me!
Me get you!
Me eat you for lunch!
Not only are you gross, but your grammar is terrible!
TRIP
Oof!

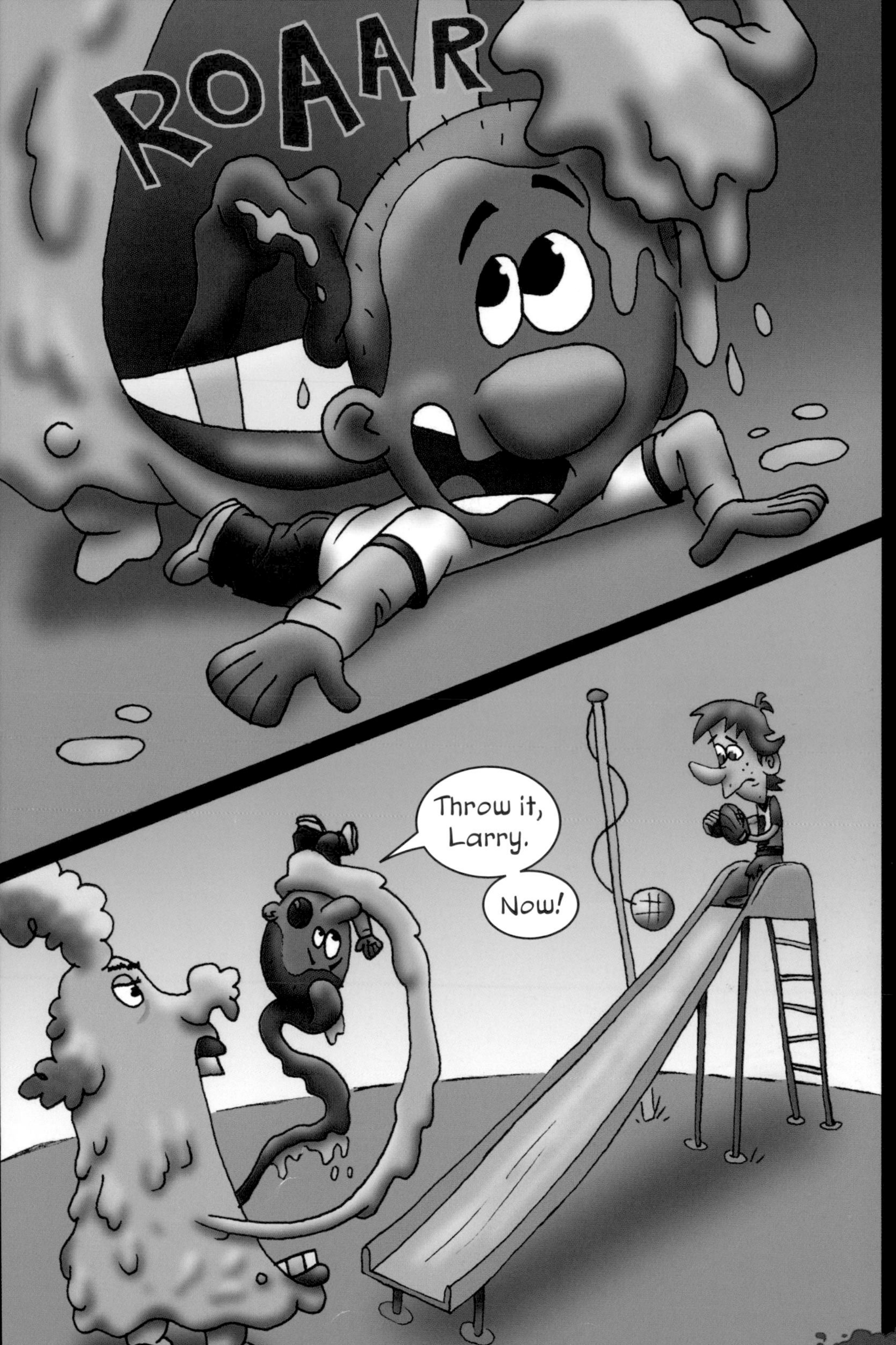
ROAAR
Throw it, Larry.
Now!

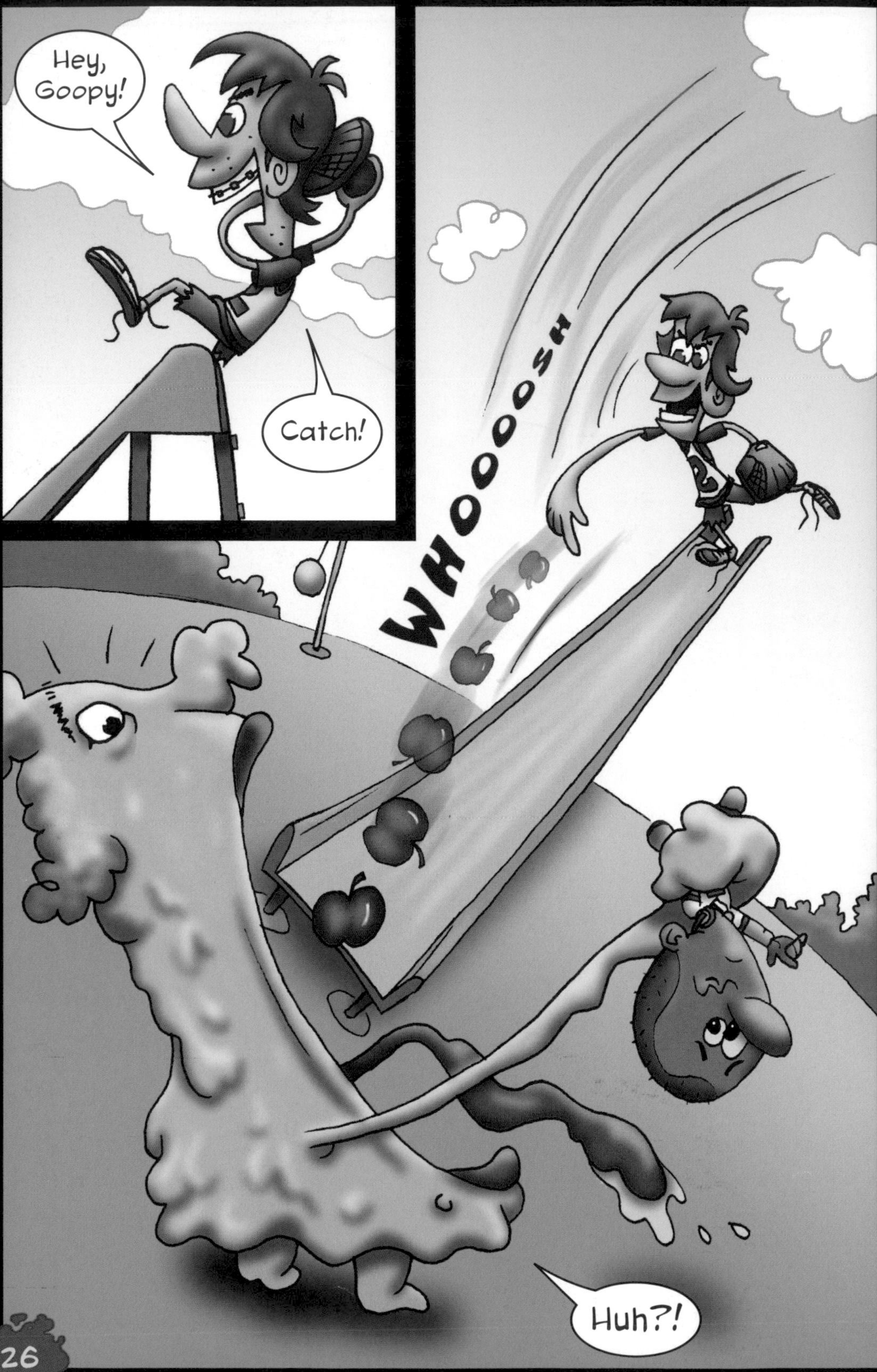
Hey, Goopy!
Catch!
WHOOOOOSH
Huh?!

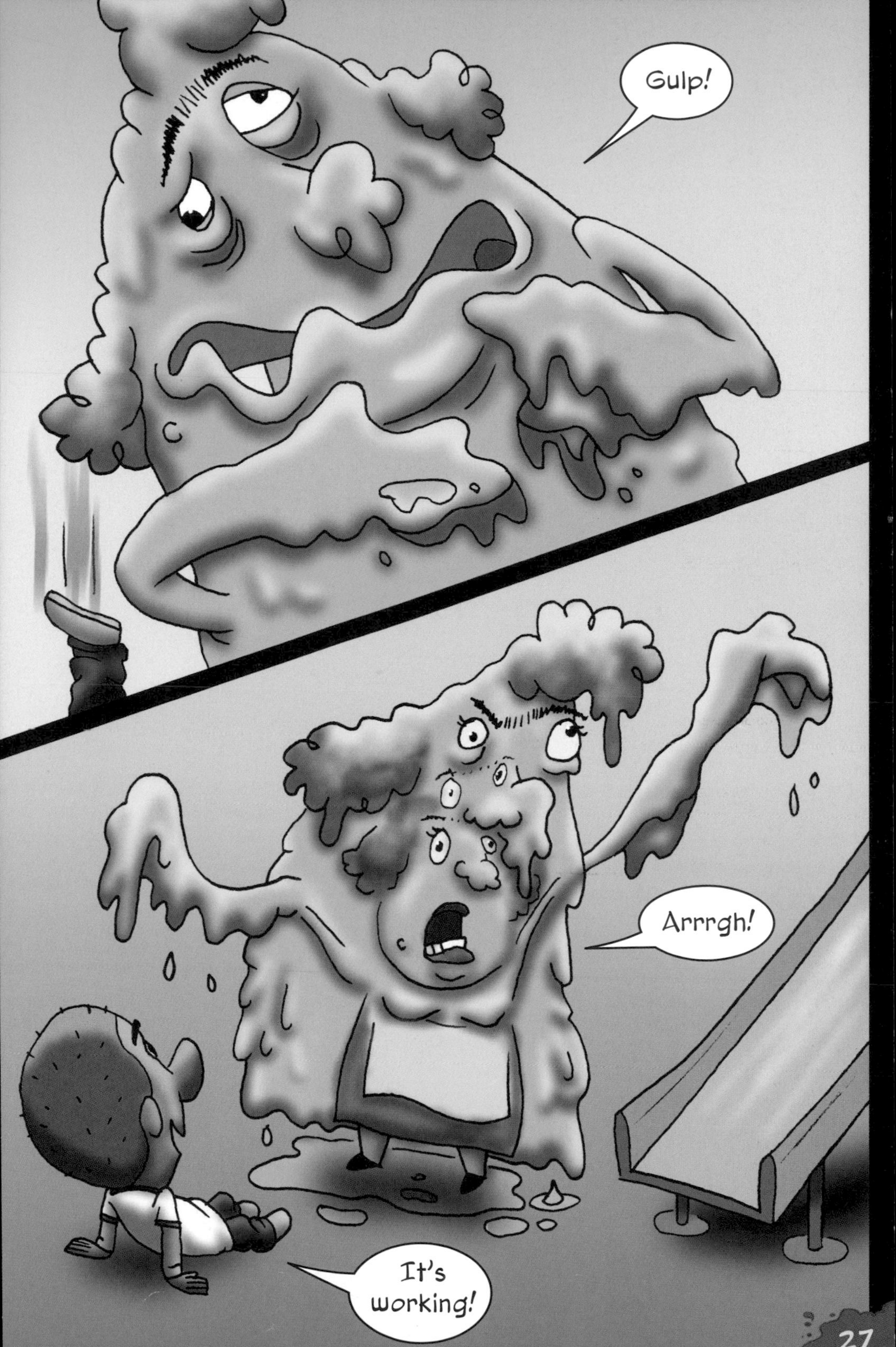
Gulp!
Arrrgh!
It's working!

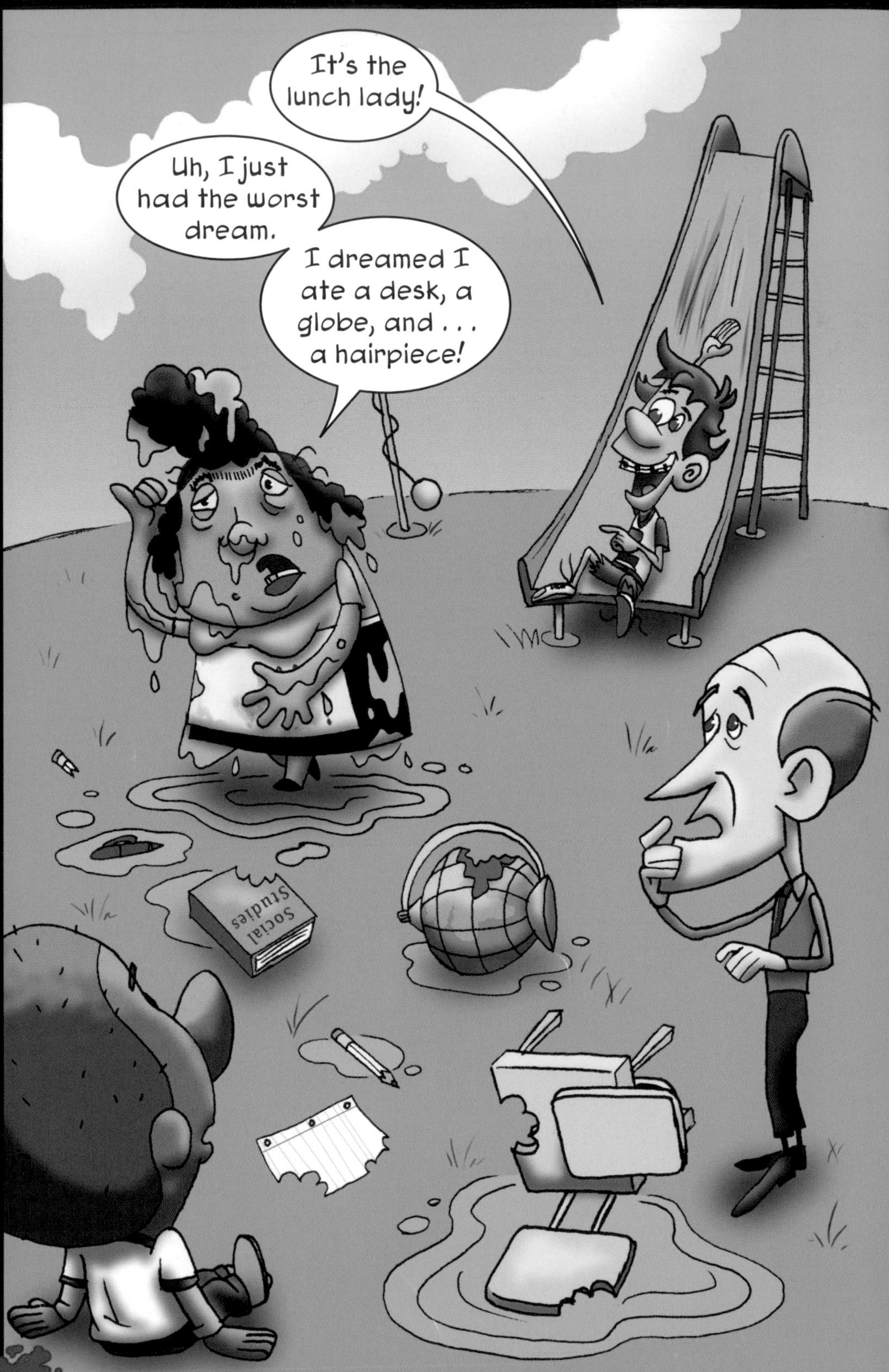
It's the lunch lady!
Uh, I just had the worst dream.
I dreamed I ate a desk, a globe, and . . . a hairpiece!
Social Studies

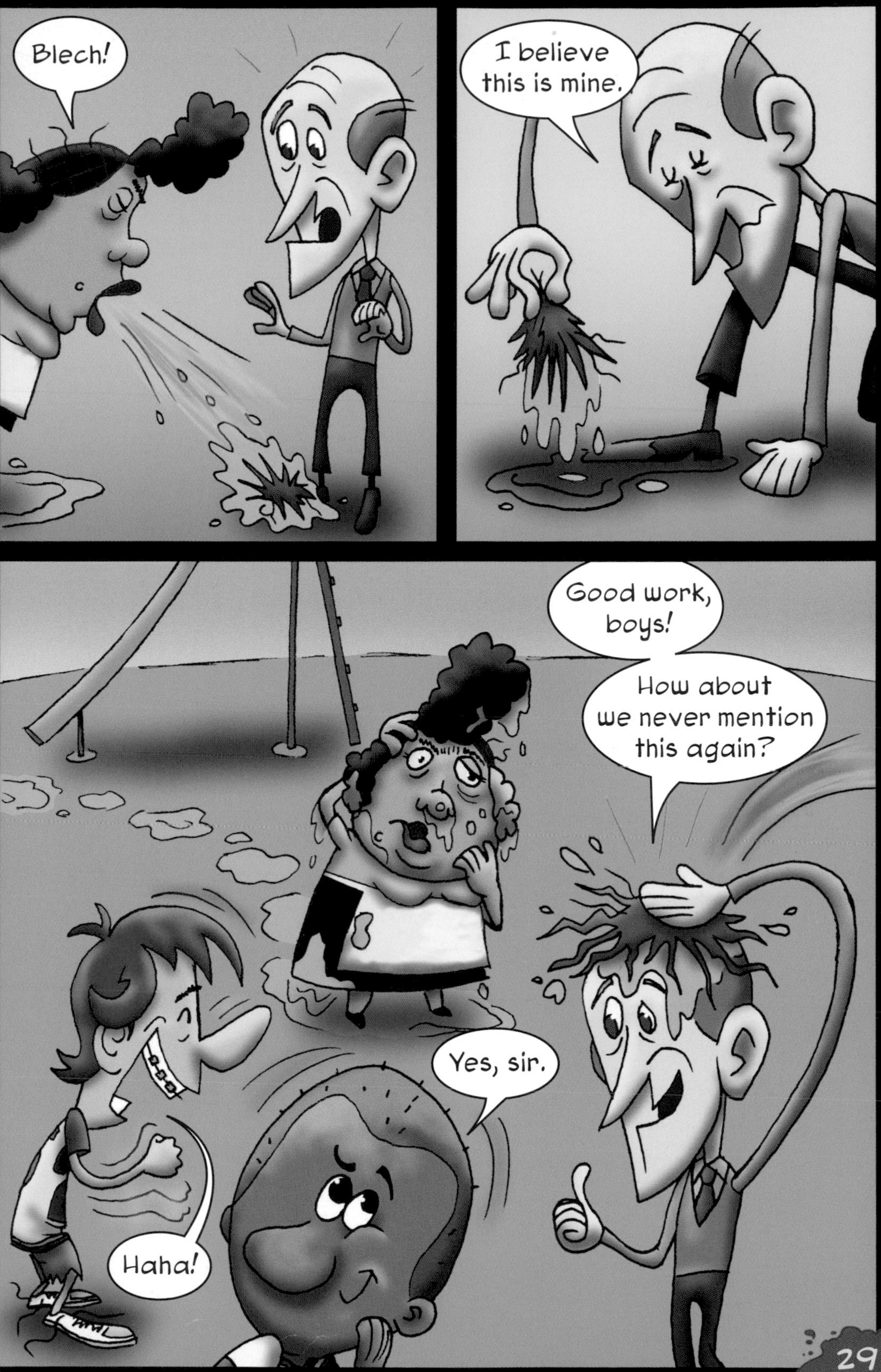

Blech!
I believe this is mine.
Good work, boys!
How about we never mention this again?
Yes, sir.
Haha!

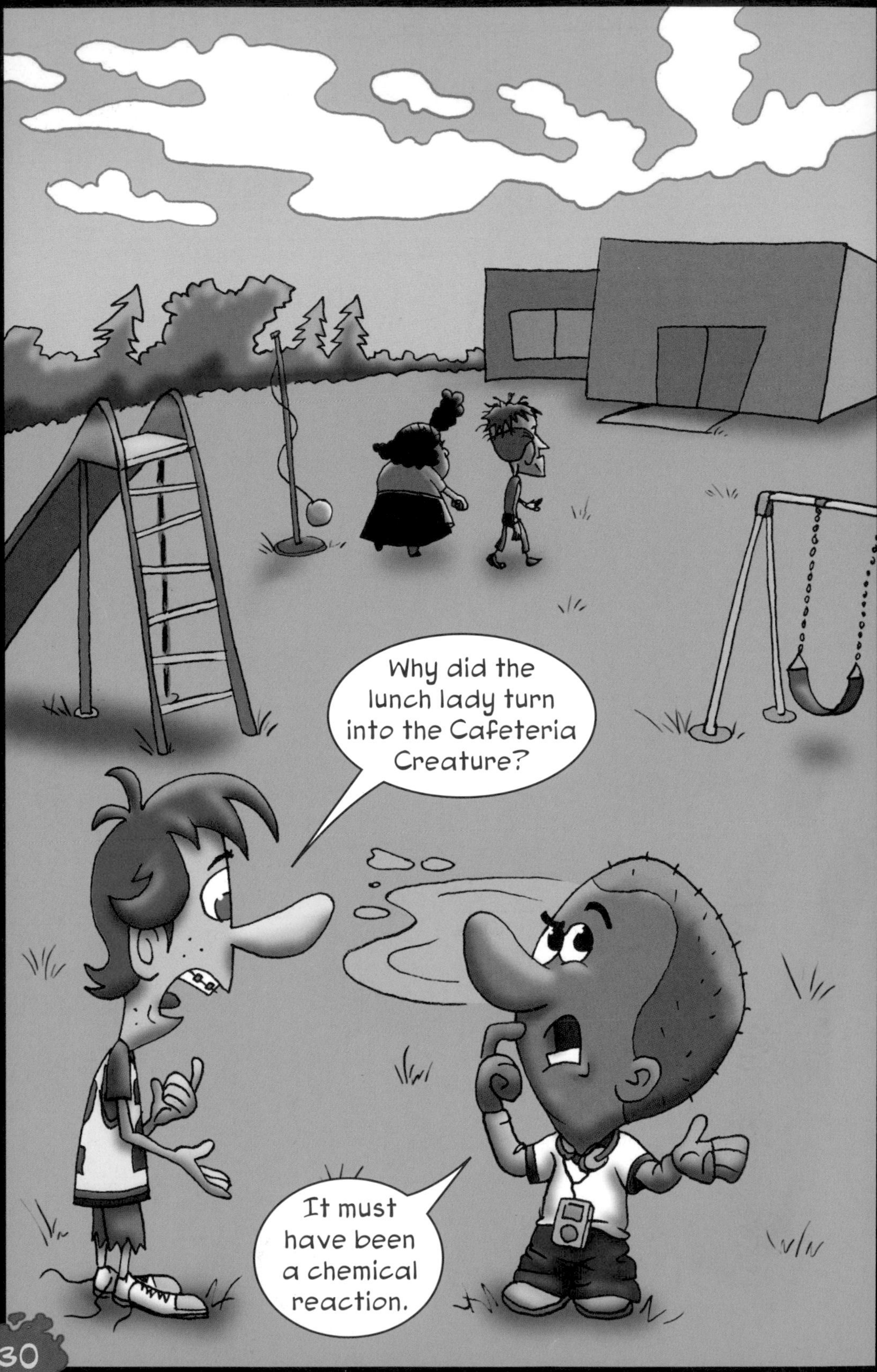
Why did the lunch lady turn into the Cafeteria Creature?
It must have been a chemical reaction.

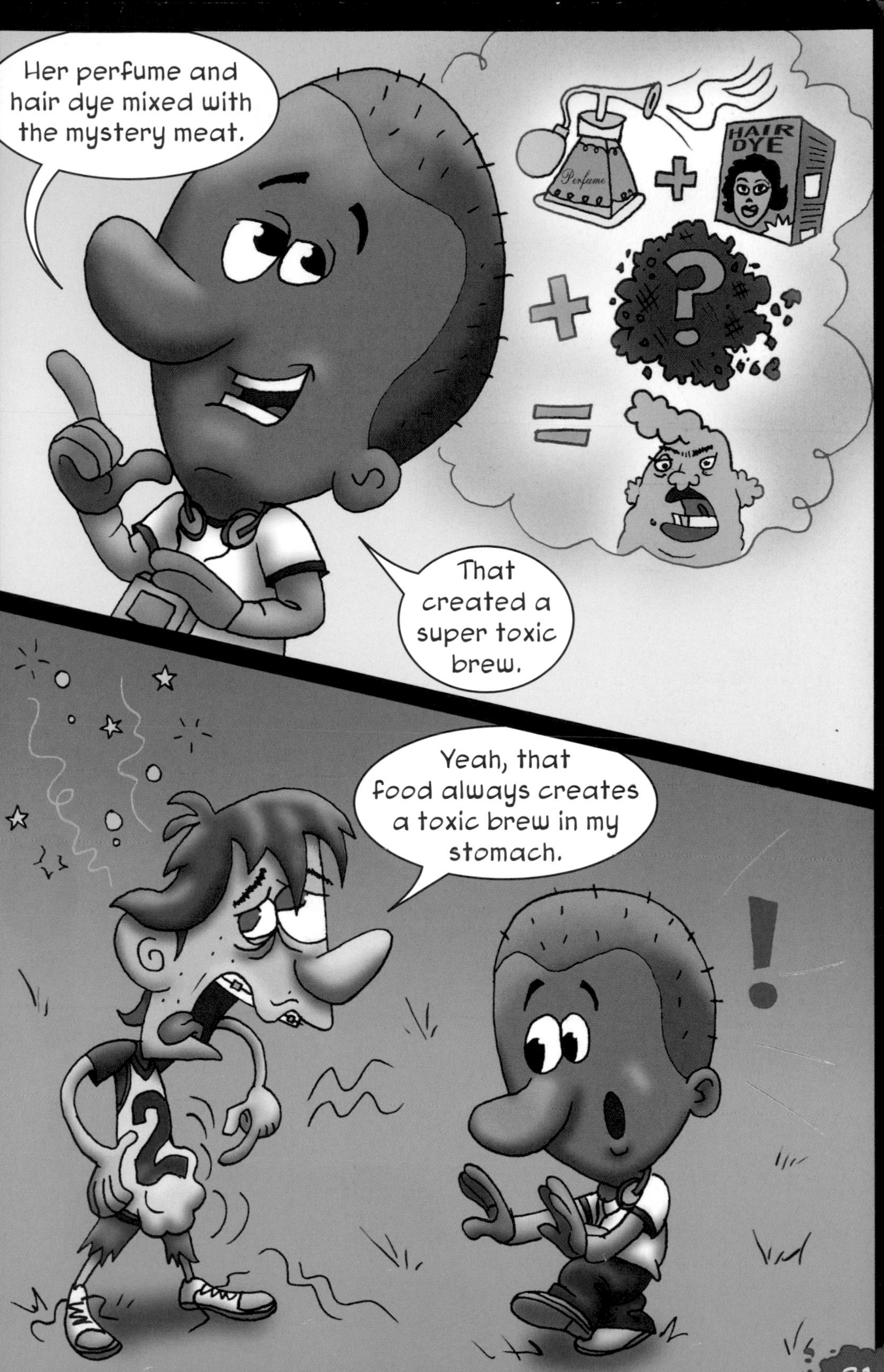
Her perfume and hair dye mixed with the mystery meat.
HAIR DYE
Perfume
That created a super toxic brew.
Yeah, that food always creates a toxic brew in my stomach.

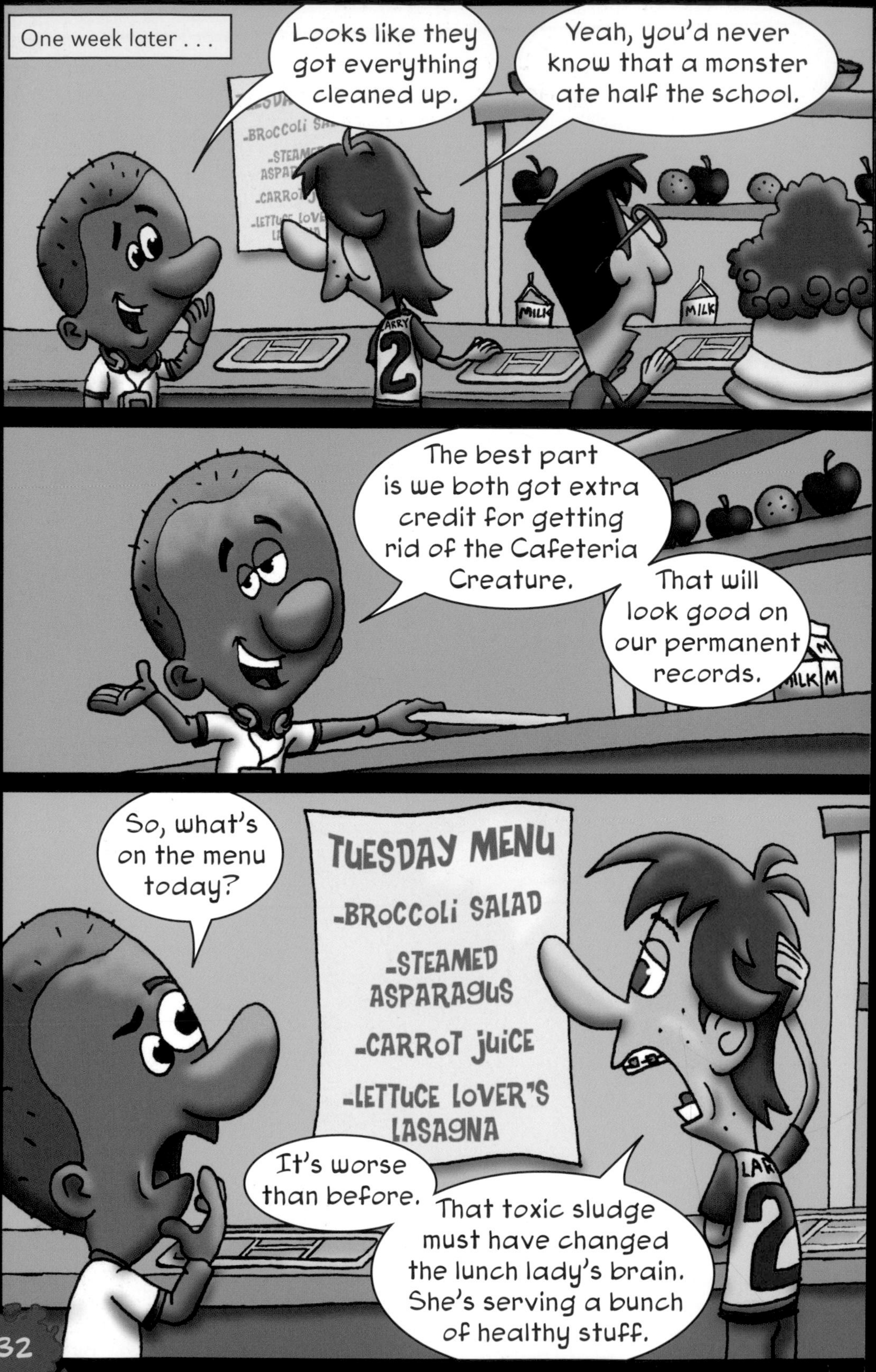
One week later . . .
Looks like they got everything cleaned up.
Yeah, you'd never know that a monster ate half the school.
The best part is we both got extra credit for getting rid of the Cafeteria Creature.
That will look good on our permanent records.
So, what's on the menu today?
TUESDAY MENU
-BROCCOLI SALAD
-STEAMED ASPARAGUS
-CARROT JUICE
-LETTUCE LOVER'S LASAGNA
It's worse than before.
That toxic sludge must have changed the lunch lady's brain. She's serving a bunch of healthy stuff.

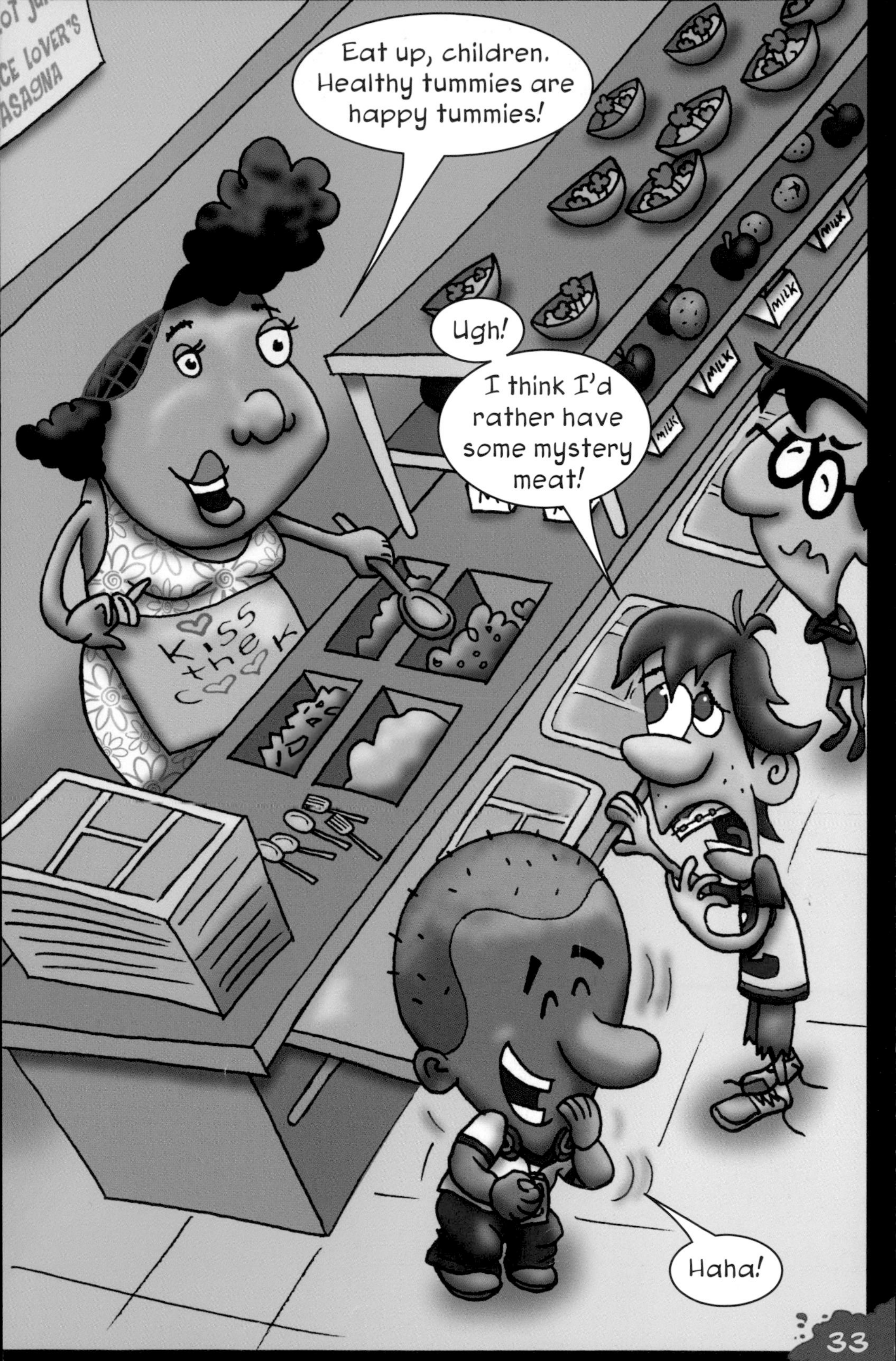
Eat up, children. Healthy tummies are happy tummies!
Ugh!
I think I'd rather have some mystery meat!
Haha!
KISS the COOK
MILK

ABOUT THE AUTHOR

Born in 1962 in Denver, Colorado, Scott Nickel works by day at Paws, Inc., Jim Davis's famous Garfield studio, and he freelances by night. Burning the midnight oil, Scott has created hundreds of humorous greeting cards and written several children's books, short fiction for *Boys' Life* magazine, comic strips, and lots of really funny knock-knock jokes. He was raised in southern California, but in 1995 Scott moved to Indiana, where he currently lives with his wife, two sons, six cats, and several sea monkeys.

ABOUT THE ILLUSTRATOR

From a young age, Andy Smith knew he wanted to be an illustrator (if he couldn't be a space adventurer, superhero, or ghost hunter). After graduating from college in 1998, he began working at a handful of New York City animation studios on shows like *Courage the Cowardly Dog* and *Sheep in the Big City,* while also working in freelance illustration. Andy has since left New York City for Rochester, NY where he teaches high school art and illustration at the Rochester Institute of Technology.

GLOSSARY

brew (BROO)—a boiling, bubbling, steaming mixture of two or more ingredients

cafeteria (kaf-uh-TEER-ee-uh)—the place where students are served food, or some type of mystery meat

chemical reaction (KEM-uh-kuhl ree-AK-shuhn)—the often dangerous response that happens when two chemicals mix

grammar (GRAM-ur)—the correct way to speak and write. This sentence ain't got no proper grammar.

hairpiece (HAYR-peess)—a wig or section of fake hair used to cover a bald spot

mystery meat (MISS-tur-ee MEET)—a mix of many unknown meats into a single dish. Hot dogs, Spam, and bologna are mystery meats (and they're not so bad, are they?).

perfume (PUR-fyoom)—a scented liquid that people spray onto their skin

permanent (PUR-muh-nuhnt)—lasting for a long, long time. Something on your **permanent** record at school will be there FOREVER!

toxic (TOK-sik)—harmful to your health

MORE ABOUT YOUR LUNCH

Some people say, "You are what you eat." Of course, they don't mean that you'll actually mutate into a mystery meat monster! But if you eat healthy foods, your body will be healthy too. Along with daily exercise, the MyPyramid plan can help you choose the right foods to keep your body at its best.

Each colored section of the MyPyramid plan represents an important food group.

Orange: Grains

The grain group includes rice, pastas, bread, tortillas, cereal, and much more. Try for whole grains if you can. They'll give you more long-lasting energy.

Green: Vegetables

Eat a variety of vegetables every day. It shouldn't be tough. There are more than 5,000 varieties of potatoes alone!

Red: Fruits

Fresh, frozen, canned, or dried, there are many ways to eat this group. Filling up on fruit should be a breeze.

Yellow: Oils

Oils come from many sources, including butter, shortening, nuts, and fish. But there's a reason this colored section is only a sliver. Only a little oil should be eaten every day.

Blue: Milk

The milk group is more than the white stuff you pour on top of cereal. This group includes cheese, yogurt, pudding, and even ice cream!

Purple: Meat and Beans

Both meat and beans have protein, which helps your body build strong muscles.

www.mypyramid.gov

DISCUSSION QUESTIONS

1. Do you think author Scott Nickel wanted the Cafeteria Creature to be funny, scary, or a little bit of both? Explain your answer.

2. What's your favorite thing to eat for lunch? Would you rather eat a cafeteria meal or bring food from home?

3. In this story, illustrator Andy Smith drew the lunch lady three different ways. Look back at the illustrations and describe how this character changed from the beginning, middle, and the end. Which version do you like the best and why?

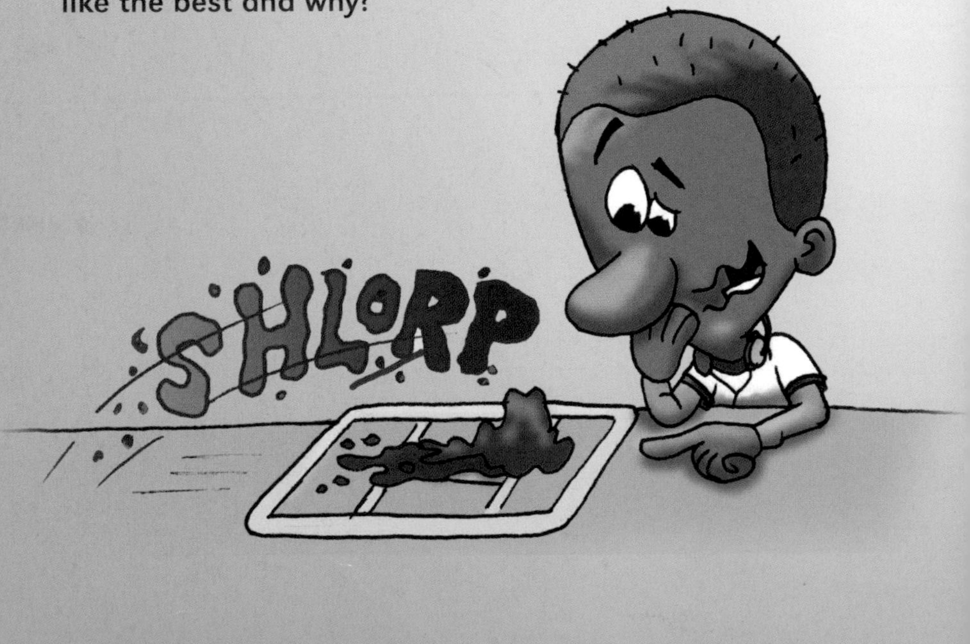
SHLORP

WRITING PROMPTS

1. Write a story about your ultimate dream lunch. If you could invite any three people in the world to join you, who would they be? What would you talk about? What would you eat for your lunch?

2. In this story, Buzz Beaker had a pretty weird day at school. Describe the weirdest, wildest, or wackiest day you've ever had at school.

3. Buzz's friend, Larry, is a really kooky kid. But in the story, we don't learn a lot about his life outside school. Write your own story about Larry's family, friends, pets, and hobbies.

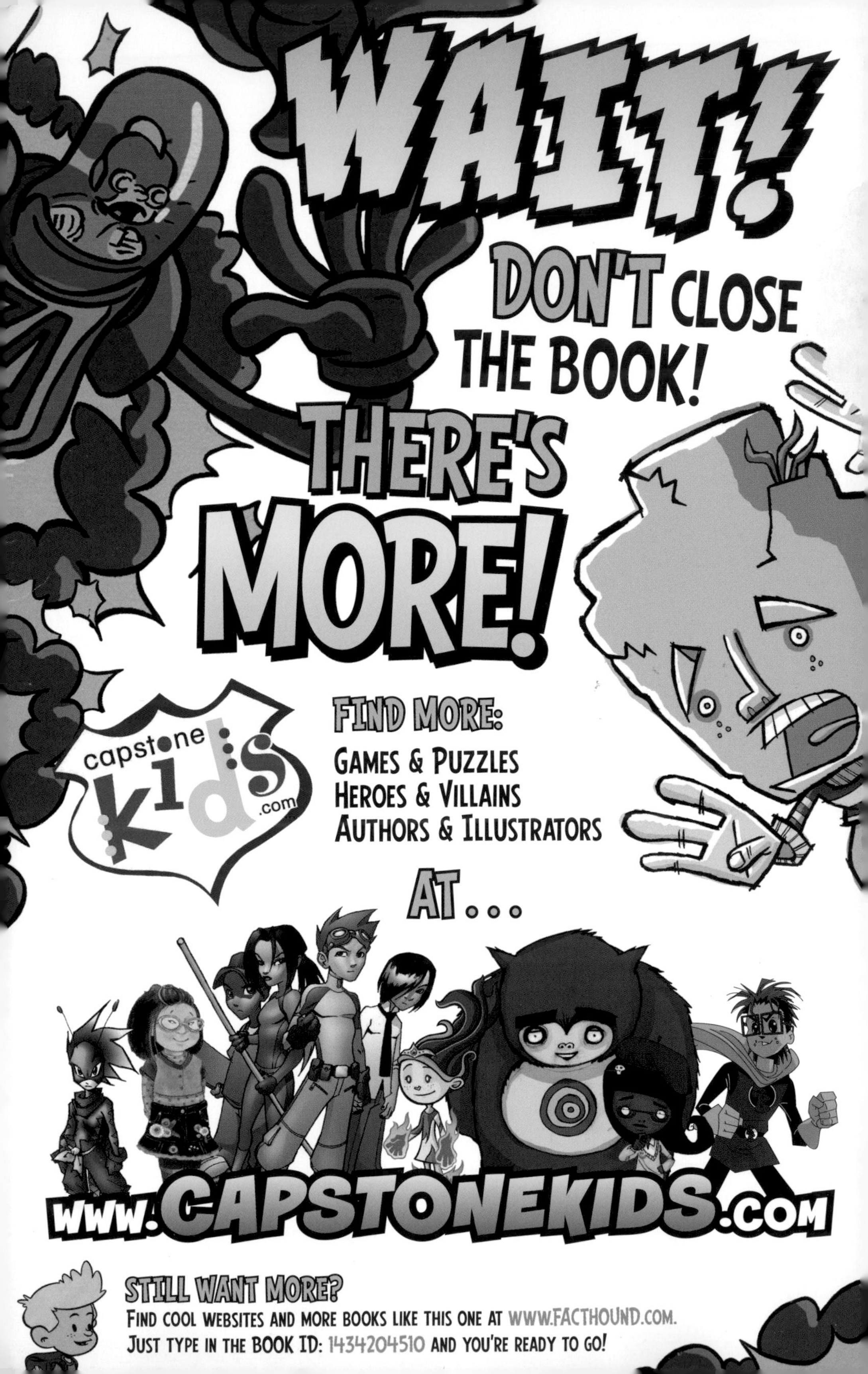
WAIT!
DON'T CLOSE THE BOOK!
THERE'S MORE!
capstone kids .com
FIND MORE:
GAMES & PUZZLES
HEROES & VILLAINS
AUTHORS & ILLUSTRATORS
AT...
WWW.CAPSTONEKIDS.COM
STILL WANT MORE?
FIND COOL WEBSITES AND MORE BOOKS LIKE THIS ONE AT WWW.FACTHOUND.COM.
JUST TYPE IN THE BOOK ID: 1434204510 AND YOU'RE READY TO GO!